GAIA'S AWAKENING
THE AVATARS OF BALANCE

TARAK

ISBN
Paperback 979-8-89929-873-8
Hardcase 979-8-89984-227-6

"Na Matu Paradevatam" – "There is no deity greater than a mother"

DEDICATION

To my beloved mother, *Bharati Bhattacharya*, who now rests with the divine. I carry her love in my heart every day, and this book is the promise I made to her—fulfilled with gratitude, emotion, and enduring memories.

To my father, *Siddheswar Bhattacharya*, for his steadfast guidance, thoughtful critique, and for questioning every element of this story—his insights made the narrative stronger, richer, and more meaningful.

To my wife, *Pampa Bhattacharya*, my silent strength, constant motivator, and unwavering supporter—her presence gives me courage and peace in equal measure.

To my daughter, *Roopsa*, my heartbeat and my universe—her boundless love and energy are my greatest source of power and inspiration.

And to my in-laws, whose faith in my talent has always lifted me—thank you for your belief, your warmth, and your quiet confidence in my journey.

A special mention of my dearest brother, my Inspirational Guru – *Surojit Kundu*, who immensely helped in reshaping this book with his wise comments & suggestions.

CONTENTS

CONTENTS

FOREWORD – THE YUGAS RETURN: A CALL TO THE SOUL

"कालचक्रं पुनरावर्तते। धर्मः स्मृतः, पुनः जागरते॥"

"The wheel of time turns once more. Dharma remembered, awakens again."

FOREWORD

In an age where the whisper of trees is drowned by the clamor of machines, and the sacred soil trembles under the weight of ambition, this book emerges like a prayer rediscovered. *Gaia's Awakening: The Avatars of Balance* is not merely a tale of myth and memory—it is a bridge across time, calling us back to the wisdom we abandoned and the Earth we inherited.

Here, legends are not locked in the past. They are breathing, evolving, reaching for us through the yugas. From the cosmic dance of Vishnu's avatars to the tender defiance of Radha, from the thunder of Narasimha to the silence of the Buddha, this narrative revives the heartbeat of divinity within the human experience.

Yet this is not just mythology—it is a mirror. Through the eyes of Gaia, we see ourselves: our triumphs, our apathy, our potential. We are the inheritors of these stories. More importantly, we are their continuation.

The author invites you not just to read, but to remember.

To return—not in retreat, but in revival. To awaken—not to dogma, but to dharma. To act—not in conquest, but in care.

As you turn these pages, you may find yourself stirred. Let it happen. Because this is not just a book—it is a calling.

And the Yuga of Awakening begins with you.

♀ PROLOGUE ♀

"यदा यदा हि धर्मस्य ग्लानिर्भवति भारत।
अभ्युत्थानमधर्मस्य तदाऽअत्मानं सृजाम्यहम्॥"

(Bhagavad Gita 4.7)

"Whenever Dharma declines and Adharma rises, I manifest Myself."

PROLOGUE: THE OATH OF THE TRIDEV

🪔 Opening Invocation

"Time: The Breath Between Worlds"

Where endings become echoes. And beginnings wait in silence.

"Dharmo Rakshati Rakshitah" (Righteousness protects those who uphold it.)

In the eternal dance of creation and destruction, the cosmos witnessed the birth of Gaia, the living soul of Earth. She was forged from the purest essence of Prakriti, woven into existence by the divine hands of the Tridev—Brahma, Vishnu, and Shiva. Her form was unparalleled, a canvas of boundless beauty, where mountains stood as her bones, rivers as her veins, and the great forests as the lush tresses that flowed across her being. She was the cradle of life, the giver, the nurturer, and the sacred mother of all beings.

But creation, in its magnificence, is never without the shadow of destruction. From the first dawn of Satya Yuga to the abyss of Kali Yuga, mankind has oscillated between wisdom and folly, reverence and defilement. The Vedas, the eternal scriptures of knowledge, forewarned of an age when men would forget their duties, when greed would replace gratitude, and when power would consume purpose.

"Yada yada hi dharmasya glanir bhavati bharata, Abhyutthanam adharmasya tadatmanam srijamyaham." (Whenever there is a decline in righteousness and an increase in unrighteousness, I manifest Myself to restore balance.)

Thus, the Tridev swore an oath—an eternal vow to protect Gaia from those who would seek to defile her. They would descend in divine forms, taking avatars to correct the course of existence, to vanquish the forces of destruction, and to renew the promise of harmony.

Each Yuga bore witness to their interventions—Matsya, Kurma, Varaha, Narasimha, Vamana, Parashurama, Rama, Krishna, Buddha—each avatar a beacon of hope in the darkness that encroached upon Gaia. Yet, as the cycle of time unraveled, the burden of sin grew heavier, the wounds inflicted upon Gaia deepened, and the arrogance of humanity knew no bounds.

Now, in the dreaded Kali Yuga, Gaia weeps, her rivers choked with filth, her forests burned in the name of conquest, and her air poisoned by the greed of those she once nurtured. Her wounds fester, manifesting in waves of destruction—earthquakes that split the earth, tsunamis that cleanse the shores, pandemics that remind humanity of its mortality. The cries of the dying are drowned by the blind pursuits of power, the quest for more, the insatiable hunger for dominion over lands and skies. But the Tridev watch in silence, their patience waning, their fury a storm yet to be unleashed.

"Maa Bhuumi Putroham Prithivyaah" (I am the child of Mother Earth.)

The Vedas teach us that we are but children of Gaia, yet we have become her executioners. The time to reform is upon us. The time to remember is now.

Mars can be explored, but Gaia must be protected first. If we are to survive, we must turn to the wisdom of the ancients, seek the harmony of nature, and learn from the stories of the past. The avatars came not just to save Gaia, but to remind humanity of its duty, of the sacred bond between creation and sustenance. For within her heart beats the essence of all that is sacred, and if she perishes, so too shall mankind.

The echoes of the past whisper through the ages—will we listen? Or shall we await the next great reckoning?

INTRODUCTION: A WHISPER FROM THE PAST

📜 Origins of Storytelling

"The Lores that Lived Before Language"

*Once, mythology wasn't read. It was received. Like rain.
Like truth.*

I come from a home where even the faintest strand of blood relation was treated with reverence and love. My parents grew up in a joint family, where the walls breathed stories, and every corner of the house echoed with the laughter, reprimands, and gentle wisdom of elders.

It was not just a family. It was an ecosystem—where grandparents, uncles, aunts, and cousins, even those from distant branches, lived, learned, and grew together. It was a home where mythology was not just a tale, but a way of life—shared at bedtime, whispered during chores, discussed in courtyards, and echoed in corrections and praises.

When we made mistakes, our elders didn't just scold us—they told us stories. Stories of gods and demons, heroes and villains, nature's fury and divine interventions. They explained virtues and vices through ancient examples—Shiva's calm rage, Rama's unwavering dharma, Krishna's strategic compassion. These stories shaped our thoughts, rewired our impulses, taught us what was right, and showed us the consequences of wrong—not through fear, but through realization.

In every word was a lesson. In every lesson, a seed of consciousness.

These values were inculcated not through lectures, but through life—in small acts, casual conversations, and family interventions. It was an unbroken tradition, a sacred oral library of Vedas, Upanishads, and Puranas, being passed from soul to soul.

As time flowed like the Saraswati River, invisible but very much present, change was inevitable.

In my generation—Gen X, the bridge between the GI generation and Millennials—nuclear families began emerging. My parents moved out for work, like many did. But we lived close to our roots. Every weekend meant a reunion with my grandparents, and festivals were grand tales come alive.

I still remember sitting in my grandfather's lap, nestled in his arms, while his voice painted vivid images of devas and asuras battling for balance. My grandmother would interrupt, laughing, "Tell him about Narasimha too!" And I would widen my eyes in awe.

But the true magic, the daily dose of divine, came every night when I snuggled next to my mother. She was no less than a modern-day Vyasa—an expert storyteller. Her voice would lull me to sleep with legends of Shiva's tandava, Vishnu's avatars, and how the earth was saved time and again by the divine.

Today, I see the world we are crafting—and I fear for it.

Micro-nuclear families are now the norm. Children grow up in isolated bubbles. Grandparents are seen once a year, sometimes only on video calls. Bedtime is owned by screens, not stories. And our rich mythology, our incredible knowledge of life, nature, balance, and self-awareness, is fading into oblivion.

This book is a small but honest attempt—an offering, a prayer—to rekindle the fire. To connect the dots for the coming generations. To help them understand how our mythology is not just history, but a mirror to our present and a guide for our future.

Every story has a purpose. Every avatar had a reason.

This book will take you through the Yugas—the grand cycle of time—and the avatars that came with them, not as fantasy, but as beacons of natural balance, intervening every time humanity veered too far from dharma.

Let us revisit the Yugas, not as distant timelines, but as rhythms of our own world, vibrating even now.

Let us look around—raging floods, devastating earthquakes, forest fires, melting glaciers, rising sea levels, and collapsing biodiversity. Is this not the Kali Yuga's crescendo?

Have we become so arrogant in our technological evolution that we cannot hear nature's cry?

Even modern science bows before the mystery of prehistoric civilizations—monuments, pyramids, temples built with unthinkable precision. Were they primitive? Or have we lost something they deeply understood?

Africa, perhaps, remains the last whisper of Eden—a continent still breathing with nature's rhythm, still connected to the pulse of life. And yet, we march on, blindfolded by machines and numbers, destroying what sustains us.

This book is a journey. A reminder. A bridge.

A wake-up call wrapped in divine tales.

Through dialogues, characters, and immersive scenes, I invite you to travel through Yugas, meet the avatars, understand their purpose, and see how nature, mythology, and human action are interwoven in a cosmic design.

Let the story unfold…

SATYA YUGA – THE AGE OF TRUTH

Time: Before time was counted. The world was new. The rivers sang with purity. The forests whispered wisdom. And dharma walked on all four legs—strong, steady, and unshaken.

"Grandfather," a young boy's voice rang out, "you said Satya Yuga was perfect. Was it like heaven?"

The old man smiled, stroking his silver beard as he looked at the fire crackling before them.

"No, child. Not heaven. But it was the closest Earth ever came to it."

In the Satya Yuga, also known as Krita Yuga, the world was drenched in truth (Satya), righteousness (Dharma), and balance. Nature and humans were in perfect harmony. There were no lies, no greed, no pollution of mind, soul, or soil. People lived long, selfless lives devoted to knowledge, meditation, and service.

Forests thrived, rivers were untouched, and even animals lived in peaceful coexistence.

In this age, there was no need for avatars—because humanity upheld dharma themselves.

But even in the purest stream, a ripple can disturb the calm.

The sages say that at the end of Satya Yuga, a faint shadow crept into the world—ego. A whisper that said, "You are greater than the world around you." And so the slow descent began.

Before the fall deepened, Lord Vishnu took the first avatar—the Matsya (fish).

THE TALE OF MATSYA: NATURE'S GUARDIAN

A great flood had been foretold.

"It will wash away everything—knowledge, life, and light," warned the Vedic seers.

And when the sky broke and the oceans rose to swallow the world, a giant fish with golden scales appeared to King Manu, who meditated by the riverside.

Matsya guided Manu to preserve the seeds of life, the sacred texts, and the knowledge of the Vedas—placing them on a boat tethered to the divine fish.

"Why save me?" asked Manu.

"Because those who carry wisdom must plant it again when the soil returns," replied Matsya, his voice echoing like the tides.

Matsya was not just a savior—it was Nature's own avatar, saving life's balance from complete annihilation. When mankind's dharma was at risk of drowning, Nature intervened.

TRETA YUGA – THE AGE OF SACRIFICE

Time passed. The Treta Yuga dawned. Dharma stood on three legs now, slightly unstable. Ego, desire, and power had grown.

Kings ruled with ambition. Rituals increased, but their essence began to fade. Nature was still revered, but exploitation had begun in the name of sacrifice.

In this age came two great avatars—Vamana and Rama.

THE TALE OF VAMANA: THE MEASURE OF GREED

"He is just a small Brahmin boy," scoffed King Bali.

The boy smiled. "Give me three paces of land."

King Bali, though a great devotee, was overreaching, extending his empire to all realms, disturbing the balance between earth and heavens.

Vamana, the dwarf avatar, measured the universe in three strides—Earth, sky, and underworld—reminding mankind: the world is not for conquest, but stewardship.

THE TALE OF RAMA: DHARMA IN ACTION

In the Treta Yuga, nature was still sacred. The forests were alive with divine energies. Rama, the ideal man and king, was born in this age.

"The forest is not exile, Sita," Rama said gently. "It is home to the rishis, the gods, and the breath of Earth."

Rama's exile through forests, his alliance with Vanaras (forest dwellers), and the battle against Ravana—the ego incarnate who abducted nature's grace (Sita – daughter of Gaia)—symbolized the struggle to protect purity and balance.

Rama stood for sacrifice, truth, and justice, even when it broke his heart.

"To protect dharma, one must sometimes walk alone," he once whispered to Lakshmana.

DVAPARA YUGA – THE AGE OF DOUBT

Dharma now stood on two legs—wobbling.

The world had become complex. Kings grew greedy. War and strategy replaced wisdom and simplicity. Nature was no longer worshipped—it was used.

In this age came Krishna, the most complex, enigmatic avatar.

THE TALE OF KRISHNA: THE COSMIC STRATEGIST

Krishna was born in a prison. A symbol of truth caged in a world of lies.

"Why do you smile even in chaos?" asked Arjuna.

Krishna looked at him and said, "Because chaos reveals truth, when you're ready to see it."*

Krishna witnessed the burning of forests (Khandava), the enslavement of the Earth by kings, and the ego of warriors who thought themselves gods.

He became the charioteer, not to drive a war, but to steer Arjuna's mind back to dharma.

The Mahabharata, the great war, was also a war for balance—where the Earth wept, and rivers turned red.

Krishna left behind the Bhagavad Gita—not just a book, but a blueprint for inner and outer harmony.

KALI YUGA – THE AGE OF DISCORD

And now… we stand in Kali Yuga.

Dharma limps on one leg, gasping.

No forest is untouched by fire. No ocean is untouched by plastic. No sky is untouched by smoke.

Children no longer hear stories—they hear sirens. Rivers do not sing—they flood. Mountains melt. Earth trembles. And humans remain distracted.

We build upward, digging downward, ignoring what lies around. The balance is broken.

We look at climate change like a distant problem. But it is the wrath of Kali Yuga—not mythological destruction, but self-made devastation.

Where is the avatar now?

Perhaps you are meant to be.

Perhaps this story, and those you will pass down, are the beginning of new dharma.

"Will there be another Vishnu?" the child asked.

The grandfather looked at the moon and said, "Maybe. Or maybe we must become the guardians ourselves. For this time, it is our actions that decide if Earth breathes again."

🐚 Chapter 1 🐚

THE BIRTH OF BEAUTY

"प्रकृतेः सौन्दर्यं जगत्स्य जननी,
गैया त्वं जीवनस्य धारा॥"

"O Gaia, mother of all that is beautiful, you are the stream of life itself."

1

THE BIRTH OF BEAUTY

In the timeless expanse of the cosmos, where stars whispered secrets to the void, the great Tridev—Brahma, Vishnu, and Shiva—gathered in divine contemplation. Their eyes shimmered with celestial wisdom as they beheld their most wondrous creation yet. Before them lay Gaia, the goddess of Earth, her form stretched across the vastness of space, breathing life into the void with her existence.

Gaia was a vision unlike any before her. Her hair flowed like the endless rivers, cascading down valleys and plains, nourishing the lands with their ceaseless embrace. Her eyes gleamed like the twin suns at dawn, reflecting the brilliance of knowledge and the serenity of nature's harmony. Her skin was a lush carpet of emerald forests, each tree a strand woven into the fabric of her being. The mountains rose from her form, majestic and eternal, standing as sentinels of time. The clouds drifted upon her breath, whispering lullabies to the slumbering lands below, and the oceans swayed like the rhythm of her heartbeat, vast and untamed.

The Tridev gazed upon their masterpiece with admiration and reverence. "Never before have we created such beauty," Brahma mused, his voice tinged with wonder.

"Indeed," agreed Vishnu, his cosmic blue skin shimmering. "She embodies balance—grace and might, peace and storm, birth and decay. She is the heart of all creation."

Shiva, the eternal destroyer and protector, nodded solemnly. "She must be guarded against those who would defile her. Any who seek to exploit her shall face our wrath."

Thus, the Tridev made a vow—to cherish and protect Gaia, to uphold the sanctity of her creation, and to punish those who sought to desecrate her splendor. Their decree echoed through the heavens, a promise carved into the very essence of existence. To ensure this, they imbued Gaia with a sacred bond, a connection that would allow them to sense her pain and rise in her defense should harm befall her.

When Gaia awoke, her celestial eyes beheld the divine figures standing before her. She gazed at them in awe, feeling the immense power that radiated from their forms. The Tridev introduced themselves with voices as deep as the cosmos, resonating through the very fabric of existence.

"Gaia," Brahma spoke, his tone rich with creation itself, "you are born from the essence of the universe, crafted with care and love. You are the soul of the Earth, destined to flourish and nurture."

Vishnu stepped forward, his presence calm and eternal. "You are the guardian of harmony, the protector of all that grows and thrives. Your purpose is to sustain life, to ensure balance in the grand cycle of existence."

Shiva's eyes gleamed with both destruction and renewal as he addressed her. "And should that balance be broken, should your sanctity be threatened, you shall rise with fury and cleanse the taint from your being. This is your duty, your purpose, your divine right."

Gaia bowed before them, accepting her destiny. She felt the immense power coursing through her, an energy that connected her to every stone, every river, and every whisper of wind.

But the gods did not stop at merely shaping Gaia's form. They adorned her with divine embellishments, as one would grace a beautiful queen with priceless ornaments. The forests were her emerald bangles, shimmering in the golden light of day. The rivers, silver necklaces that flowed with unbroken grace, adorned her body. The mountains stood like majestic crowns, glistening with the purest snow, while the vibrant flowers that bloomed across her plains were the delicate jewels that added brilliance to her already resplendent form. The celestial sky became her veil, embroidered with countless stars, casting an ethereal glow upon her being.

Moved by their devotion, they granted Gaia the greatest gift—a fragment of their divine power. "With this," Brahma declared, "you shall weave life from the essence of your love."

Gaia, now imbued with divine might, closed her eyes and exhaled, her breath carrying the first whispers of life. From her rivers and oceans emerged creatures of endless forms, from the tiniest fish to the grandest beasts. From the depths of her forests arose the creatures of land, swift-footed, wise-eyed, each a testament to her boundless affection.

But it was from the very soil of her being that she molded her most cherished creation—humans. Formed with care, she imbued them with the ability to think, to feel, to love. She gazed upon them with maternal pride and whispered, "You are my children. Honor this land, for it is of me, and I of it."

The Tridev watched as Gaia's children spread across her body, their feet kissing the earth with every step. They rejoiced in her bounty, danced in her rain, and sought wisdom in her mountains. For a time, harmony reigned, and the earth flourished in its divine splendor.

But the Tridev knew that there would come times of darkness, moments when mortals would falter, when forces beyond their understanding would threaten the harmony they had crafted. To prepare for such moments, they devised a secret way to ensure that Gaia would always have protectors—beings forged from both divine and earthly essence.

Together, they planted sacred seeds within the most fertile depths of Gaia, hidden in the purest rivers, the tallest mountains, and the deepest forests. These seeds carried the essence of the Tridev themselves, waiting to awaken in times of need. From these seeds, extraordinary beings would arise—Avatars, champions who would walk among mortals, bearing the power and wisdom of the gods.

"These Avatars shall be the guardians of balance," Vishnu declared. "They will descend upon the earth in times of great peril, guiding mortals and restoring harmony."

"They shall carry our strength," Shiva added, "and wield the fury of destruction should the land be defiled."

"And they shall be wise," Brahma concluded, "with the knowledge of creation itself, to lead with compassion and foresight."

Thus, the Tridev ensured that Gaia would never stand alone. She would always have her protectors, her warriors of light, born from the secret power sown deep within her being.

But time is an ever-turning wheel, and the seeds of discord lie hidden in the shadows of prosperity. Little did Gaia or the Tridev know, a storm was brewing—a storm that would test their vows, shake the heavens, and awaken the wrath of the very Earth they had sworn to protect.

Chapter 2

THE DAWN OF SATYA YUGA AND THE FIRST AVATAR

"मत्स्यरूपेण गहने वेदानुद्धृत्य पावनः।
सत्ययुगे जगन्नाथः, जलान्ते स्वर्गव्रज॥"

"In the form of a fish, the sacred knowledge was retrieved; in the Satya Yuga, Heaven touched the seas."

2

THE RISE OF MANKIND AND THE DAWN OF SATYA YUGA

Time: Before the world knew division. Before desire had a name. The universe, freshly woven, pulsed with clarity. Dharma stood with four feet planted firmly, steady like the roots of an ancient banyan. This was Satya Yuga, the Age of Truth.

The air was crisp with purity. The rivers sang lullabies of clarity. Forests weren't just homes for beasts—they were temples, breathing sanctuaries of spirit and breath. Gaia walked among her creations unseen but ever-present. Her whispers lived in the rustle of the leaves, her sighs carried by the wind.

In this age, humanity was still young—innocent, connected, and attuned to the natural rhythm of the cosmos. The sun and moon were not feared but revered. Mountains were mentors, and rivers were sisters. There were no temples carved in stone yet, because every tree, every stream, every stone was divine. Meditation was instinctual. Compassion was the norm. The idea of conquest did not exist.

Families lived with purpose, tribes in harmony. They spoke not just in words, but in the rhythms of nature. One could tell the hour by the birdsong, and the seasons by the flavor of the wind. Knowledge passed through the breath, from elder to child—not in script, but in soul. Wisdom was a lived experience. It flowed like a gentle stream—never forced, always offered.

The people of this age were deeply connected to the five elements—earth, water, fire, air, and space. They didn't just live on the land; they lived with it. Offerings were made to the rivers before bathing, to the trees before taking fruit, to the air before uttering sacred chants. Every action was aligned with cosmic rhythm.

But even perfection quivers under time's shadow.

A disturbance emerged—a slow, silent corruption, like ink bleeding into pure water. A demon named Hayagriva, maddened by ambition, dove into the cosmic ocean and stole the Vedas. The sacred texts—life's blueprint—were lost to the abyss. The world darkened. Wisdom was silenced. The cosmic rhythm faltered. The chants of sages turned to cries of despair.

Gaia cried out. Her forests echoed her sorrow. Without the Vedas, without knowledge and balance, mankind would falter. And so, her cry reached Vaikuntha.

Vishnu stirred.

"The song of the Earth is silent," he murmured. "She is forgetting her own breath."

A shimmer lit the cosmos as Gaia appeared before him, radiant yet wounded, her essence flickering like a fading flame.

"I can no longer carry this alone," Gaia said, voice trembling. "The weight of forgetting has dulled even my oldest rivers."

Vishnu rose and approached her, arms wide, not in dominion, but in embrace. "Then let us carry it together. Let us renew what was always meant to be eternal."

She stepped into his arms, and their divine energies spiraled, interlacing light with soil, breath with water, purpose with potential. The cosmos watched in reverence as the two converged—not as lovers alone, but as twin flames of sustenance and salvation. From their celestial union, Matsya was born—his form rising like starlight from ocean mist, golden-scaled and luminous.

THE TALE OF MATSYA: THE TIDE OF RESTORATION

On the banks of a quiet river, King Manu knelt in meditation. A seeker of truth, his heart was open to the whispers of the divine. That night, as stars bathed the sky, a tiny fish appeared in his cupped palms.

"Protect me," it spoke.

Manu gasped. "Who are you, sacred one, to speak in the tongue of men?"

"I am a voice of the cosmos," the fish replied. "Care for me, and I shall reveal more."

Startled, yet filled with wonder, Manu placed the fish in a bowl. It grew overnight, outgrowing every vessel—bowl to pot, pot to tank, tank to river. Until finally, Manu led it to the ocean.

And there, the fish transformed—towering, radiant, divine.

"You are Vishnu!" Manu fell to his knees. "Why did you come in this form?"

"Because the world needs to be preserved through the very waters that now threaten it," Matsya replied. "A flood will come—a deluge to cleanse the corruption that festers. Gather seeds of every life. Bring the sages. Bring the Vedas. Build an ark."

"And who will guide us?" Manu asked.

Matsya lowered his horn. "Tie your ark to me. I shall lead you through the storm."

Manu obeyed. As the heavens cried and oceans roared, he sailed the floodwaters, tethered to the horn of the mighty Matsya. Beneath the waves, Vishnu battled Hayagriva, reclaiming the Vedas, restoring the light.

Their battle shook the deepest corners of existence. Hayagriva hissed with pride, wings cutting through the void, eyes burning with greed. But Vishnu, in his aquatic glory, glided like liquid justice. Their clash was thunder and silence combined—waves cracked like glass, and Gaia held her breath.

The ark floated for days uncounted. The sages within sang hymns to preserve memory. Seeds lay bundled in sacred cloth, whispering their intent to sprout once more. Aboard the vessel, Manu meditated through storms and silence alike. He knew this was not an end, but a beginning disguised in chaos.

One night, under the stillness of stars, Manu whispered, "Matsya, what will become of mankind after this deluge?"

The divine fish answered, "They shall begin again. But remember, Manu—forgetfulness is the first fall. Tell your descendants the stories. Keep memory alive."

As the demon was vanquished and the Vedas lifted once more into the world, a golden light bathed the ocean depths. From this light, sages emerged, carrying seeds, scrolls, and whispers of memory. Vishnu handed them back to humanity, not as a possession, but a sacred trust.

When the waters receded, the land was fertile once more. Trees sprang from the mud. Rivers resumed their song. Birds returned to their nests. The animals stepped onto land not with fear, but with reverence. The sun returned not just as warmth, but as blessing.

The cycle had restarted. Balance, for now, was restored.

But Gaia knew—this was only the beginning. For even those who listen may one day forget. And the forgetting would come with a cost.

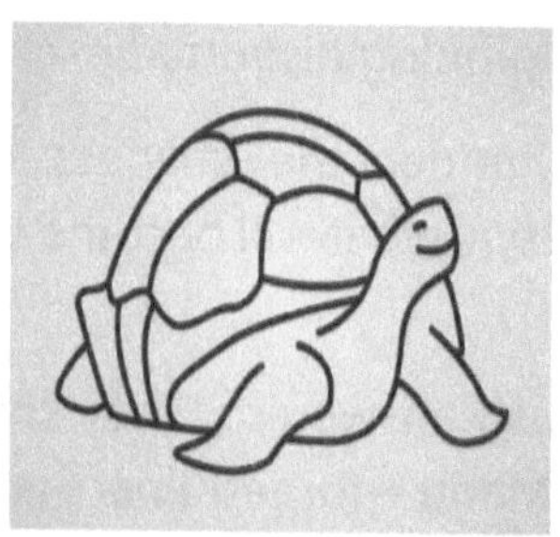

🐢 ☄ Chapter 3 🐢 ☄

THE KURMA AVATAR

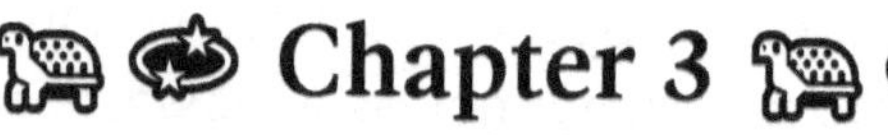

"कूर्मवपुषा धारयामास मेरुं,
मन्थनशक्त्या सृजति जीवनम्॥"

"With the form of a turtle, he bore the cosmic mountain; through the churning, life emerged."

3

THE CHURNING OF DESTINY

Time: The cycle turns. Treasures lie hidden. Desires now have form. Power has a taste.

The cosmic ocean of Kshirsagar churned with potential and promise. Beneath its frothy tides lay Amrit, the nectar of immortality—an ancient essence that could tip the balance of existence. The Devas, weakened from battles with the Asuras and burdened by dwindling strength, grew desperate. Their light flickered. Their dominion wavered.

But the Asuras were growing stronger, their ambitions rising like untempered fire.

And so, born of desperation, an uneasy pact was made—Devas and Asuras, eternal foes, would churn the ocean together to retrieve the nectar. It was a partnership forged not from trust, but necessity. The promise of Amrit was more tempting than the memory of betrayal.

Mandara, the great mountain, was chosen as the churning rod. Vasuki, the serpent king, was summoned as the rope. Yet the moment the churning began, chaos unfurled. Mandara, though mighty, could not remain afloat. The mountain began to sink into the ocean's abyss.

Panic erupted among the Devas.

"We are losing it!" Indra cried.

"The mountain must be steadied," shouted Varuna. "Or the ocean will devour us all!"

High above, Gaia watched, her pulse agitated, her waters bruised by the violence. The ocean, once her song of serenity, had become a cauldron of greed.

"They churn not to balance, but to possess," she whispered in sorrow.

And then, she called.

THE BIRTH OF KURMA

Vishnu heard her.

From the stillness of Vaikuntha, he stepped into meditation upon Ananta Shesha. His eyes closed, his breath in rhythm with Gaia's tremors.

"They have forgotten to honor the base that holds the divine," he said.

"Then you must become it," Gaia replied softly. "Let your back carry what their hands cannot."

With their spirits entwined, Vishnu summoned his essence downward, deep into the waters of the cosmos.

From their union—her burden, his resolve—emerged Kurma, the Great Cosmic Tortoise.

He rose from the depths slowly, ancient and serene, his shell inscribed with sacred symbols that shimmered with starlight. His body was the balance of time itself—solid, still, enduring.

The gods gasped.

"A tortoise?" asked Agni.

"A foundation," answered Brahma, his voice reverent.

Kurma descended beneath Mandara, his back perfectly curved to cradle the mountain. The ocean calmed as his shell anchored creation itself.

"Climb, churn, pull," Kurma whispered. "I shall bear the world."

The churning resumed.

The Devas took one side of the serpent. The Asuras the other. Vasuki hissed, his coils tightening, his breath spewing poison into the heavens.

Mount Mandara spun atop Kurma's back like a golden spindle. Waves crashed. Thunder cracked. And from the depths, gifts began to surface—treasures long lost in the folds of time.

Kamadhenu, the divine cow of abundance

Airavata, the white elephant, massive as thunderclouds

Ucchaishravas, the seven-headed horse

Kaustubha, the jewel of purity

Kalpavriksha, the wish-fulfilling tree

And then, Lakshmi, the goddess of beauty and fortune, rising like dawn from the foam

The gods rejoiced. The ocean shimmered with miracles.

But then, the ocean darkened. A bubbling, black venom spilled forth—Halahala, the poison that could unmake the world.

The Devas staggered. The Asuras recoiled. Even Kurma held his breath.

From Mount Kailash, Shiva descended.

"This venom shall not take what we have restored," he declared.

He drank the poison in one breath. Parvati held his throat, her divine touch containing its spread. His skin turned blue. The universe paused to honor the one who consumed death to save life.

Finally, Amrit rose.

Golden. Pure. The nectar of gods.

The Asuras lunged for it, hungry with ambition. But Vishnu, assuming the form of Mohini, danced before them—ethereal, entrancing, divine illusion.

"Let me serve you, O warriors," she smiled. "Let me offer you the drink of immortality."

Blinded by desire, the Asuras agreed. And while entranced by her charm, she handed the nectar only to the Devas.

One Asura, Rahu, disguised himself and sipped the nectar. But the sun and moon saw him, exposed him. Mohini struck him down—his head and body cursed to chase the sun and moon forever, causing eclipses.

The churning ended. Balance was restored. The ocean calmed.

Below, Kurma remained still, unwavering.

Vishnu appeared before him.

"You may rest now," Vishnu said.

Kurma smiled, his eyes deep with cosmic silence.

"Let them forget who churned. Let them forget who drank. But may they never forget who bore the weight."

Gaia reached toward him, her presence brushing his shell.

"You did not just carry Mandara," she said softly. "You carried me."

And Kurma, the silent guardian, sank once again into the depths—his back bearing the unseen burdens of the world.

But above, Gaia knew: the churning had stirred more than nectar. It had awoken ambition in its sweetest form—disguised as victory, hidden as pride.

"What comes next," she whispered, "will not churn water… but hearts."

But even as the celestial order was reaffirmed, the cycle of time turned once more. The forces of darkness would rise again, and when they did, another avatar would emerge, forged from divine purpose, destined to protect Gaia once more.

   # Chapter 4

THE VARAHA AVATAR

"वराहरूपेण महीं समुद्धत्य,
अन्धकारं प्रज्वलयामास॥"

*"As Varaha, he lifted Earth from darkness,
igniting light in the void."*

4

THE ONE WHO DEFIED THE ABYSS

Time: The demon rises. The Earth falls.

Gaia had known darkness. She had endured floods and poison. But this time, the void was different. It was not chaos. It was silence. An aching, smothering stillness that pressed into every crevice of her being. The oceans did not sing. The skies did not weep. They waited.

Hiranyaksha, the asura of unparalleled strength and unrelenting arrogance, had declared war not just on the Devas, but on balance itself. In his thirst for dominion, he had seized the Earth—**Gaia herself**—and hurled her into the abyss of the cosmic ocean. With every push deeper into darkness, he severed her from the celestial harmony she nurtured.

"Let her drown in silence," he bellowed. "Let the gods grieve her absence."

And so, Gaia sank. Her mountains shuddered. Her rivers coiled in on themselves. Her forests grew still. Her heart, the pulse of life, slowed.

But in her fading breath, she called.

THE BIRTH OF VARAHA

High in Vaikuntha, Vishnu stirred. Seated upon Ananta Shesha, he felt her cry ripple through dimensions—not as sound, but as sorrow.

"She falls," he said softly. "Not from height, but from hope."

He closed his eyes. The universe dimmed. Gaia's essence reached out, fragile and flickering. With solemn purpose, Vishnu drew in her pain and kindled his resolve. He did not descend as a sage. Nor as a man. But as an ancient force of instinct and might.

From their divine convergence—his promise and her need—rose Varaha, the Great Boar. Massive. Primeval. Sacred.

His form crackled with divine energy. His tusks curved like crescent moons of justice. His roar shattered the silence between stars. Where his hooves touched, dimensions trembled.

The Devas gathered, stunned.

"Is that a beast?" Agni whispered.

"No," said Brahma. "That is the foundation of protection. That is Varaha."

And Varaha dove.

The celestial oceans parted at his command. As he descended, realms blurred. Layers of existence peeled back like petals. The currents tried to slow him. The shadows whispered doubts. But Varaha surged forward.

In the abyss, Gaia drifted—dimmed but not broken. Her body chained by Hiranyaksha's dark magic, her roots frozen in time. Yet her eyes flickered open.

"You came," she said. Her voice, barely a breath.

"Always," Varaha rumbled, swimming closer.

Chains hissed, tightening as Hiranyaksha emerged from the gloom.

"Another god in skin of fur?" the asura mocked. "Come to drown with her?"

"I come to raise what you tried to bury," Varaha replied.

The battle was instant and immense. Fists met tusks. Roars collided with silence. Every blow echoed through the ocean floor. Currents became whirlpools. Coral crumbled. Fish fled.

Gaia watched, her heart rekindling with each surge of Varaha's strength. The boar god glowed brighter with every strike, his body radiating the will of creation.

"You fight for a dying world," Hiranyaksha screamed.

"No," Varaha thundered. "I fight for the one that gives life."

With one final charge, Varaha impaled the demon upon his tusks. Hiranyaksha shrieked, flailing as his form disintegrated into shadow. The waters calmed. Silence returned—but it no longer smothered. It sighed.

Varaha approached Gaia gently. His tusks lowered. His voice softened.

"Hold on to me," he said.

Gaia wrapped her essence around him, and with divine strength, Varaha ascended. Higher and higher. The ocean bowed away. Light seeped in. Stars aligned. Planets watched.

As they breached the surface, Gaia blinked against the sunlight. Birds sang. Clouds formed halos. The world held its breath.

Varaha walked upon the surface of the sea, each step forming new land. With care, he placed Gaia upon the sacred platform of existence once more. Mountains rose. Rivers unfurled. Forests breathed.

He knelt beside her, pressing his tusks into the soil.

"You remember me?" she asked, a tear of rain gliding down her cheek.

"Until the end of time," he whispered.

She exhaled. Her breath became wind. Her smile summoned dawn.

Above, the Devas rejoiced. Below, the demons hissed in fury. But Gaia knew, balance had returned. For now.

She looked to Vishnu, who now stood in his divine form beside her.

"You came not with wrath," she said, "but with a roar that remembered love."

"Because wrath cannot raise," Vishnu replied. "Only love can lift what has fallen."

Yet even as life returned, a shadow lingered. Not from strength. Not from silence. But from cunning.

"They will not always strike with fists," Gaia whispered. "One day, they will strike with words. With illusions. With cleverness."

Vishnu nodded.

"And when that day comes, I shall return again. Not as boar. But as lion."

And Gaia, reborn, stretched her arms across the world. Mountains stood taller. Waters glistened. Seeds cracked open.

But the memory of the abyss remained within her—etched like a scar. For she knew, in the tapestry of yugas, darkness was never gone.

It only waited.

But the cycle was not yet over. Darkness still lurked in corners unseen, and the balance, though restored, remained fragile. The gods watched, knowing that the time would come when Vishnu must rise again, in yet another form, to stand against the tides of destruction.

The saga of the Avatars was far from over.

 Chapter 5

THE NARASIMHA AVATAR

"नृसिंहदेवो नृहरिर्देवशत्रोः विनाशकः।
दिव्यकोपः धर्मसंस्थापकः॥"

*"Narasimha, destroyer of tyrants, divine rage
embodied, restorer of Dharma."*

5

THE ROAR FROM THE PILLARS

Time: Midst of Treta. Dharma walks on two legs. Pride no longer hides in shadows. It wears crowns.

The world had risen again after darkness. Gaia breathed once more. Her forests thickened with age-old wisdom. Rivers swelled with songs of life. Yet a new darkness grew—not from beneath, but from above. It descended from palaces, cloaked in silk and gold, spoken through decrees etched in fear. It came in the form of Hiranyakashipu, the asura king.

He was no mere conqueror. He was the sculptor of fear. Cities burned in his wake. Sages fled into silence. Even the Devas, once fierce, watched from afar. The heavens themselves withheld intervention.

For Hiranyakashipu had secured a boon, woven with loopholes no weapon could penetrate:

- ✦ Not by man or beast.

- ✦ Not during day or night.

- ✦ Not indoors, not outdoors.

✦   Not by weapon or by hand.

He proclaimed himself god. He ordered temples razed. He demanded Gaia herself bow to him.

She did not.

Gaia, though battered, stood firm.

"He poisons the breath of my forests," she whispered. "His pride chokes my skies."

And yet, from the root of his own bloodline, a spark of resistance flickered.

Prahlada, his son, a boy born of fire and faith, worshipped Vishnu.

"There is one who breathes life into all," the child said.

"Where is this god of yours?" the king roared.

"Everywhere," Prahlada replied calmly. "Even in this pillar."

The king's eyes burned. The palace trembled with his rage. And then—

With a cry of hatred and disbelief, he struck the pillar with his mace.

THE BIRTH OF NARASIMHA

The blow echoed through the pillars of time.

The pillar cracked—not as stone, but as **womb**. For Gaia, the Earth, held the pillar in her belly. She had become the altar of this divine birth.

A fierce wind roared. The skies darkened. Thunder clapped though no clouds gathered. And from the fracture of Gaia's stone soul, something ancient emerged.

NARASIMHA.

He was a storm given flesh. Half-lion, half-man. Fully divine.

His eyes did not blink—they burned. His mane lashed like a thousand whips of fire. His claws curved like scimitars carved from suns. Each breath growled through the realms.

"Who dares call himself god?" he thundered.

The palace shattered. Courtiers fled. Hiranyakashipu stumbled backward, eyes wide.

"What—what are you?!"

"I am balance," Narasimha snarled. "Born of Gaia's cry and Vishnu's promise."

He moved like thunder, swift and terrifying. He seized the king at the hour of twilight—neither day nor night. Upon the threshold—neither inside nor outside. With claws, not weapons. With wrath, not hand.

"You dared desecrate Earth's breath," Narasimha growled, holding the asura aloft. "Now she shall watch you fall."

And with a roar that silenced gods, Narasimha tore the tyrant apart.

Limb from limb. Bone from bone.

Blood bathed the courtyard. The skies howled with his fury.

It was not justice alone—it was divine reckoning.

The world trembled. Forests crouched in submission. Oceans stilled. Even the stars dimmed their shine, afraid to blink.

Prahlada, kneeling, wept—not in fear, but in awe.

Narasimha stood tall, body heaving, eyes searching. But the threat was gone. The pride vanquished.

And yet, his fury remained.

"Calm yourself, my Lord," Prahlada said softly. "You have restored the rhythm."

But Narasimha's roar still rumbled. His claws still gleamed.

Even gods struggle to silence the storm born from dharma wronged.

Then Gaia rose. Not as stone, nor soil, but as spirit— radiant, emerald, alive.

She stepped through the blood-soaked wind and stood before the lion. She did not flinch. She did not tremble. She embraced him.

"You have torn the lie," she whispered. "Let truth breathe again."

He snarled. But her scent was soil and sapling. Her touch was monsoon and mountain. And slowly, he softened.

His breath slowed. His claws dulled. His eyes dimmed to gold. From the heat of divine rage, Vishnu stepped forth, returned to calm.

"I did not roar to destroy," he said. "I roared to awaken."

Gaia laid her hand on his chest.

"Then stay near. The next darkness will not wear a crown. It will wear a smile."

Vishnu nodded.

"I shall return—as teacher, as wanderer, as warrior. But always, as balance."

The skies cleared. The stars sang.

Gaia stretched across the lands again. She whispered Narasimha's name to the trees, the rivers, the winds.

She told the world not of a lion who killed—but of a lion who came when dharma screamed.

And in temples built generations later, people still whisper to the pillar:

"He came from here."

Not from heavens. Not from stars.

But from the Earth—

From Gaia.

Chapter 6

THE VAMANA AVATAR

"त्रैविक्रमेण पृथिवी त्रैणीकृता धर्मेण।
वामनः पादेन आच्छादयत् लोकाः॥"

*"With three strides, Vamana covered the worlds, restoring
Dharma through humility."*

6

THE THREE STRIDES

Time: The end of Treta. Dharma leans on two legs and a cane. Pride, though once shattered, now disguises itself as generosity.

The Earth had seen destruction. She had seen justice roar through Narasimha. But Gaia now faced a new shadow—not of brute force or deception, but one that walked in robes of sanctity and wore crowns of generosity. This was not the age of warriors alone. This was the age of ambition dressed as piety.

The golden radiance of Satya Yuga had dimmed. The age of unblemished truth had ended, giving way to the Treta Yuga—the Silver Age. Gaia, who had once flourished in perfect harmony, now bore the scars of human ambition.

The rivers still flowed, but their waters carried the weight of desire. The forests stood, but their roots trembled under the burden of greed. The once selfless devotion of mankind had turned inward, and kings sought dominion not just over their lands, but over the heavens themselves.

Gaia sighed, her breath rippling through the winds that carried whispers of war and conquest. She felt the tremors beneath her surface—men who once walked in reverence now marched with weapons, fueled by hunger for power.

Yet, she did not despair!

She had known this cycle would come. As virtue waned and arrogance grew, the divine forces that had vowed to protect her would rise once more.

Among the mortals, one name echoed with both reverence and fear—Mahabali, the Asura king of great might and greater ambition. Unlike his demonic forefathers, Mahabali was not cruel. He ruled with wisdom and justice, and his people flourished. Yet, his heart carried the seed of unchecked pride, and that seed grew into an unquenchable thirst for supremacy.

Through countless battles and conquests, he extended his dominion across the earth. But it was not enough. His gaze turned upward, beyond the mortal realm, to the very heavens. He sought to claim what was never meant for one of flesh and blood—to rule over the Devas themselves. Gaia shuddered, feeling the weight of his arrogance pressing upon her.

The gods convened. Indra, whose throne trembled under Mahabali's growing power, turned to Vishnu. "If he ascends, the balance will break. The worlds will be thrown into chaos. Something must be done."

Vishnu listened, his cosmic eyes scanning the great expanse of existence. He had known this day would come. He turned his gaze toward Gaia, and in her sorrowful silence, he found his answer. Balance must be restored, but not through war. This time, wisdom would triumph over might.

Thus, Vishnu descended once more—this time, in the form of a child. The Vamana Avatar was born.

THE DIVINE TRICKSTER ENTERS THE COURT OF MAHABALI

The court of Mahabali was a place of splendor, adorned with gold and marble, echoing with the voices of poets and sages who sang praises of their king's greatness. It was in the midst of this grandeur that a small figure appeared.

A Brahmin boy, no taller than a child of five summers, with radiant skin that shimmered like molten gold, stood at the entrance. His eyes, deep as the cosmos, held an ancient wisdom that belied his youthful form. Clad in simple saffron robes, he walked barefoot upon the cold stone, yet the air around him hummed with unseen power.

Mahabali, ever the gracious ruler, rose from his throne. "Welcome, young Brahmin. You stand in the court of Mahabali, where no guest leaves empty-handed. Ask of me what you wish, and it shall be yours."

Vamana smiled, his small hands folding in respectful greeting. "Great King, your generosity is known across the worlds. I seek but three paces of land, measured by my own steps."

Laughter erupted through the hall. Ministers and warriors exchanged amused glances. Three paces? From a boy so small? Surely, this was no request worthy of a king's attention.

Yet, Mahabali raised a hand, silencing them. "You ask for so little, child. Why not ask for gold, for cattle, for a kingdom?"

Vamana's gaze did not waver. "He who is content with little has no need for excess, O King. Grant me this, and I shall be satisfied."

Mahabali, ever the noble ruler, nodded. "So be it." He picked up the sacred water to seal the promise.

Shukracharya, his wise guru, stepped forward, his voice laced with urgency. "My King, wait! This is no ordinary child. I sense the divine within him. He is Vishnu in disguise! If you grant his wish, you will lose all you have built."

Mahabali hesitated, but then smiled. "If it is the will of Vishnu, then so be it. I would rather lose everything by my own word than break a promise given in good faith."

With that, he poured the water, sealing the pact.

THE ASCENT TO THE COSMOS

The moment the sacred droplets touched Gaia, the air thickened with power. A great silence fell over the court as the small boy began to change. He grew—his body expanding, stretching beyond the palace walls. His feet crushed the marble beneath them, his head pierced the clouds, and his arms spanned the sky. The laughter of the courtiers turned to gasps of awe and terror.

Mahabali could do nothing but stare as the being before him, no longer a child but the infinite form of Vishnu, raised his foot and took the first step.

With one stride, Vamana covered Gaia complete. She looked too small to his feet.

With the second, he traversed the vast heavens, reclaiming the dominion that Mahabali had sought.

Then, he turned to Mahabali. "You promised me three paces, O King. The earth and heavens are mine. Tell me, where shall I place my final step?"

Mahabali, realizing the divine will at play, knelt before Vishnu. "Place it upon my head, Lord, and let me return to the depths from where my ancestors came."

Vishnu smiled. He placed his final step upon Mahabali, pressing him gently into the netherworld, not as a punishment, but as a ruler granted his own dominion beneath the earth.

Yet, so moved was Vishnu by Mahabali's selflessness that he granted him a boon—the right to return once a year to visit his people, in a festival that would be celebrated as Onam, a reminder of a king's great heart.

THE CYCLE CONTINUES

Gaia felt the weight of conquest lift from her shoulders. Balance had been restored once more. Yet, she knew this peace would not last forever.

For even as the Silver Age progressed, men would continue to hunger for power. Kings would rise, and with them, darkness. And when the balance tilted again, the gods would return.

The cycle was unbroken, and Gaia, ever watchful, awaited the next test.

Vishnu had come as the wise child, but next, he would return as the warrior prince. The age of righteousness would soon be challenged by tyranny, and with the dawn of the next avatar, the world would witness the fury of the mighty Parashurama.

✑ Chapter 7 ✑

THE PARASHURAMA AVATAR

"परशुहस्तः क्षत्रदर्पनाशकः,
धरणीपुत्रः पुनरुद्धारकः॥"

*"Wielding the axe, the pride of kings he cut; Earth's savior,
he rose from the soil."*

7

THE WRATH OF THE AXE

The Treta Yuga had unfolded like a grand tapestry, woven with both light and darkness. While righteousness still had its place, shadows of corruption crept into the hearts of men. Kings who were once noble had turned arrogant, wielding their power like a sword against their own people.

The Kshatriyas, the warrior class, had become tyrants rather than protectors. Their greed consumed the lands, their egos towering higher than the mountains. Gaia, once lush and thriving, was now tainted by the blood of the innocent, her rivers thick with the cries of the oppressed.

The sages, who once meditated in peace, now feared for their lives. Dharma was crumbling, and the sanctity of the earth teetered on the edge of destruction. Gaia wept, her pain echoing through the cosmos. The Tridev heard her sorrow, and once again, Vishnu prepared to descend to restore balance. This time, his fury would manifest not in kindness or patience, but in divine retribution.

THE BIRTH OF THE WARRIOR SAGE - PARASHURAMA

Deep in the ashrams of the sage Jamadagni, a child was born to his wife, Renuka. From the moment he took his first breath, the earth trembled, and the skies roared with approval.

Vishnu had manifested himself again as Parashurama, the warrior sage, destined to wield the divine axe and purge the world of its corruption.

From a young age, Parashurama exhibited strength beyond measure and a mind sharpened by wisdom. Under his father's guidance, he mastered the Vedas and the arts of war. His body became a vessel of discipline, honed by years of meditation and relentless training. The gods themselves watched in awe as he grew into an indomitable force, his heart burning with the fire of righteousness.

One fateful day, his father's ashram was desecrated by a band of arrogant Kshatriya warriors. They laughed at the sage, mocked his simple life, and, in their cruelty, slaughtered his sacred cow, Kamadhenu. When Jamadagni pleaded for justice, they responded with steel, striking him down without remorse.

Parashurama's world shattered. The weight of his father's lifeless body in his arms ignited a fury so fierce that even the heavens shuddered.

His hands clenched around the handle of his axe—a weapon gifted to him by Shiva himself. The divine blade gleamed, thirsting for the blood of the corrupt. With a single stroke, the first of many tyrants fell, their arrogance drowned in their own crimson tide.

THE WAR AGAINST THE CORRUPT

The Kshatriyas had long believed themselves invincible. Their fortresses stood tall, their armies vast. But none could stand against the wrath of the one who bore the axe. Parashurama moved like a storm across the land, his strikes precise, his fury unmatched. He waged war for generations, his vengeance relentless.

Twenty-one times he cleansed the earth, twenty-one times he vanquished the oppressors who had defiled Gaia. Kingdoms fell, palaces burned, and rivers ran red with the sins of the fallen.

Yet, even as he struck down the unworthy, Gaia whispered to him. Her voice was gentle, pleading. "My son, you have restored balance, but the earth weeps for peace. The cycle of destruction must end."

Parashurama, drenched in the blood of those who had defiled dharma, finally understood. The purpose of his wrath had been served, but vengeance could not be the foundation of a new world. He laid his axe to rest, retreating to the mountains to meditate, his duty fulfilled.

THE LEGACY OF PARASHURAMA

Though his war had ended, his legend lived on. The axe-bearer would not perish but would remain, an eternal force in the world, watching, waiting for the moment he would be called upon again.

As Treta Yuga stretched forward, kings and warriors spoke his name with reverence and fear. They knew that should arrogance and tyranny rise again, so too would the one who had once cleansed the earth twenty-one times over.

Gaia, now bathed in the silver glow of Treta Yuga's wisdom, sighed in relief, knowing that should the balance falter again, her warrior son would return. But even as peace prevailed, the cosmos whispered of the trials yet to come.

The time of the great Ram was drawing near, and the earth would once again need its savior. The saga of Vishnu's avatars was far from over.

  # Chapter 8  

THE RAMA AVATAR

"रामो विग्रहवान् धर्मः, सीता जगज्जननी।
रावणान्तकं पुण्यकर्म, तेजस्वी सत्यव्रतः॥"

*"Rama is Dharma incarnate, Sita the Earth Mother; their
story a luminous vow of truth."*

8

THE SCION OF DHARMA

Time: The dawn of Dvapara. Dharma staggers forward, supported by memory and myth. Gaia aches not from war, but from neglect, betrayal, and silence.

As the Treta Yuga aged, the burden upon Gaia grew heavier. The world, once pristine and harmonious, began to crumble under the weight of unchecked desires and arrogance. Kingdoms flourished, but so did tyranny. Power, instead of being wielded for the welfare of the people, became an intoxicant that drove men to war, deceit, and cruelty. The rivers ran red with blood, and the cries of the oppressed reached the heavens. Gaia, once abundant and nurturing, now bore the scars of devastation wrought by the very children she had once loved.

From her depths, she sent her agony skyward, a silent plea for salvation. The Tridev heard her cry.

Vishnu, the Preserver, the eternal force of balance, knew his next descent was imminent. Evil had manifested in the form of Ravana, the ten-headed tyrant who had subjugated the world under his might, defying the very laws of dharma. His arrogance knew no bounds; he had grown so powerful that he believed himself invincible, even to the gods themselves. Gaia shuddered at the weight of his misdeeds, and the cosmos trembled with the need for justice.

Thus, Vishnu chose his next form—the perfect man, the embodiment of righteousness, the torchbearer of dharma. Born into the illustrious Ikshvaku dynasty, he would be known as Rama, the prince of Ayodhya.

THE BIRTH OF RAMA

In the grand kingdom of Ayodhya, where the Sarayu River flowed with an eternal serenity, King Dasharatha and Queen Kaushalya were blessed with a son, a child radiant with divine energy. The moment he took his first breath, the world seemed to pause. Flowers bloomed in unseasonal abundance, the skies rained petals, and the heavens resounded with celestial hymns.

Brahma himself whispered to Gaia, "Your protector has arrived."

Rama grew into a prince unlike any other—wise beyond his years, disciplined in mind and body, and, above all, bound to the sacred path of dharma. He wielded his bow not as a weapon of conquest, but as an instrument of protection. Every action, every word, every breath of his being radiated righteousness.

Gaia watched him with hope, for she knew that in his hands lay the future of her restoration.

The winds of time had carried the echoes of avatars past—roars, thunder, cosmic paces. Yet now, a different kind of savior was needed. Not one who would fight with weapons, but one whose very presence would nurture balance, restore forgotten truths, and awaken a sleeping world.

Gaia called out—not in desperation, but in invocation. "Let her rise from me," she whispered to Vishnu. "Let her walk not as wrath, but as grace."

And Vishnu, seated upon Ananta Shesha, listened with solemn eyes. "The Earth suffers not from demons alone," he said, "but from the absence of the divine feminine. She needs her Shakti."

THE BIRTH OF SITA

Before Ravana rose, before the great war that tore Lanka from the sky, there was a calm before the storm—a time when Gaia prepared her guardian.

From the deepest folds of her heart, Gaia pressed a prayer into the sacred soil of Mithila. Not with flames, but with fertility. Not with sound, but with sanctity.

"She shall not be born through blood," Gaia vowed. "She shall be born through remembrance."

In the kingdom of Mithila, King Janaka performed a yajna to end a long drought. As part of the sacred ritual, he took up the golden plough himself—a gesture of humility and prayer.

Each furrow in the Earth was a call to divinity. Each turn of the blade an offering of service.

AND THEN—THE EARTH TREMBLED.

His plough struck something soft, resonant, unlike rock or root. He knelt. Dug with trembling hands.

There, wrapped in layers of loam and glow, lay a baby—not crying, not afraid, but watchful, radiant.

A hush fell over the land.

The winds paused. The rivers stilled. The sun bowed.

"A daughter," Janaka breathed. "A daughter gifted by Gaia herself."

He named her Sita—from the Sanskrit *Seet*, the furrow. She was the line drawn in Earth by a king, answered by a goddess.

SITA, THE EARTH-BORN FLAME

Sita grew not like other children. She didn't learn the Earth—she remembered it.

She would speak to trees and receive answers. Flowers bloomed in her palms. Birds sang differently when she passed. Animals would pause in reverence.

Her beauty was not of this world.

- ✦ Her eyes shimmered with compassion deeper than oceans.

- ✦ Her skin glowed with the golden tint of river-silt.

- ✦ Her voice could lull storms.

✦   Her smile bent warriors to their knees.

Every prince in every direction sought her hand. But none could draw Shiva's bow, for she was not meant to be won—she was meant to be *understood*.

And when Rama arrived, the Earth paused.

Two souls born of dharma. Two lights cast for one path.

She looked into his eyes and saw not a man—but a mission. He looked upon her and saw not beauty—but balance.

Their union was not mere marriage. It was **Gaia's prophecy fulfilled**.

THE KNOWING WITHIN HER

Unlike others, Sita always knew.

From the moment Janaka lifted her from soil, she remembered Gaia's whisper.

"You are born not to rule, but to remind. Not to conquer, but to connect."

In exile, she did not weep. In forest, she did not fear. In Lanka, she did not falter.

When Ravana tried to tempt her with wealth, palaces, and praises, she stood unshaken.

"You think power seduces me?" she asked. "I was born from the breast of the Earth. I have held storms in silence. You cannot move me."

And when Agni held her in flames, he could not burn her.

For she was not fire's enemy—she was its twin.

THE FALL OF DHARMA - THE RISE OF RAVANA

While Rama grew under the guidance of sages, in the distant land of Lanka, Ravana tightened his grip upon the world. Born of a great lineage yet consumed by unchecked ambition, he had once been a devout scholar, a devotee of Lord Shiva. But power had twisted his soul. He no longer sought wisdom—he sought dominion over all creation. He conquered lands, subjugated kings, and even dared to defy the heavens.

Gaia recoiled from his presence; wherever his feet tread, the land withered, and the rivers dried. He plundered sacred groves, enslaved sages, and shattered temples. His greatest sin, however, was his belief that he was above dharma itself.

When his tyranny reached its peak, he set his sights upon Sita, the beloved wife of Rama. The moment he laid eyes upon her, he desired her, not out of love, but as a conquest to prove his supremacy. With deceit and treachery, he abducted her, wrenching her from Rama's side, carrying her away to the golden towers of Lanka. Gaia screamed in sorrow, for the abduction of Sita was the final wound, the ultimate violation of balance.

THE WAR FOR GAIA'S HONOR

Rama, broken yet resolute, vowed to rescue Sita. But more than that, he vowed to rid the world of Ravana's darkness. Gathering an army of vanaras, the noble Hanuman at his side, he marched upon Lanka. The ocean itself bowed before him, parting to allow his forces passage. Gaia, emboldened by his resolve, whispered through the winds, through the rustling leaves, through the roaring tides—this was her champion.

The battle that ensued shook the very core of existence. Lanka, once golden and resplendent, became a battlefield where gods and demons clashed. Every arrow released from Rama's bow carried the weight of divine justice. Hanuman, the mighty warrior, tore through the enemy ranks like a storm incarnate. The earth trembled as Ravana's monstrous armies fell.

Ravana, enraged yet unshaken, emerged from his palace, his ten heads towering like mountains, his twenty arms wielding weapons of unearthly power. He roared, his voice splitting the skies, "No man can kill me! No god can defeat me! I am the master of my fate!"

But Rama was neither just a man nor a god—he was dharma itself, manifested in flesh. With a calm that could silence storms, he faced Ravana. "You have defiled Gaia, you have defied the laws of the universe, and for that, justice shall find you."

The battle between Rama and Ravana was unlike any other. Every blow shattered the sky, every clash of their weapons sent shockwaves across the land. The heavens darkened as their energies collided. Rama fought with the grace of the divine, each movement precise, each strike a declaration of fate. Gaia, wounded but watching, prayed for her protector's victory.

Finally, as the war neared its climax, Rama invoked the ultimate weapon—the Brahmastra, the arrow of celestial wrath. He aimed at Ravana's navel, the source of his immortality, and with a whisper to Gaia, released it. The arrow blazed through the air, carrying the weight of truth, the power of the cosmos, and the vengeance of the oppressed. It struck true, and Ravana fell, his reign of terror ending in an inferno of divine justice.

SITA'S ROLE IN SAVING GAIA

The battle of Lanka was not just Rama's victory. It was Gaia reclaiming her voice.

Through Sita, the Earth reminded kings that strength must kneel before sacrifice, that love must be held like a promise, not a possession.

Even in her final moments—when Rama doubted, when society turned its eye—Sita returned to her mother.

She stepped onto Gaia's soil and whispered:

"If I have lived with truth, let the Earth accept me."

The Earth split. Gaia rose—not as soil, but as sanctuary. She took Sita back—not as loss, but as light returned.

And the world knew once more:

That sometimes, avatars rise not with swords, but with silence. Not with power, but with purpose. Not to rule, but to remember.

Sita, the daughter of Gaia, had done what no war could—she had shown the world that the feminine divine is not just support.

She is source.

THE RESTORATION OF BALANCE

With Ravana's fall, Gaia exhaled. The air grew lighter, the rivers flowed freely once more, and the land, once parched by tyranny, began to heal. Rama reunited with Sita, but even in his victory, he upheld dharma above all. The trials did not end with the war; they continued, as his love for Sita was tested, his rule questioned, and his righteousness scrutinized.

Yet, he remained steadfast—a king not of power, but of duty.

His reign, known as Ram Rajya, became the golden age within the Treta Yuga—a time when justice, honor, and harmony reigned supreme. Gaia flourished under his rule, her scars healing under the touch of a just ruler.

But as the cycle of time moved forward, the seeds of darkness would once again take root. Treta Yuga, despite its splendor, carried within it the seeds of Dvapara Yuga.

The world would once again tip towards imbalance, and when that time came, Vishnu would descend once more. This time, as Krishna, the enigma, the strategist, the divine force of cosmic play.

Thus, the Treta Yuga neared its twilight, and the echoes of a new age whispered upon the winds, calling forth the next great saga—the Dvapara Yuga had begun.

🎻📄 Chapter 9 🎻📄

THE KRISHNA AVATAR

"वासुदेवः सर्वं इति,
गीतामृतं लोकरक्षायै॥"

"Vasudeva is all; the Gita's nectar was poured for the world's salvation."

9

THE KEEPER OF DHARMA

THE DAWN OF DVAPARA YUGA

Time: The descent of Dvapara. Dharma limps through the labyrinth of illusion. Gaia mourns not just from destruction, but from deception—brother turns against brother, and the sacred soil drinks the blood of its own protectors. The battlefield is no longer distant—it is within the hearts of kings.

As the Treta Yuga faded, its echoes of righteousness and sacrifice grew dim, giving way to the Dvapara Yuga. The Silver Age had now tarnished, its luster diminished by the weight of human ambition. Kings and rulers, once the guardians of dharma, now sought power for their own gain. Gaia trembled beneath the burden of greed, her forests stripped for palaces, her rivers tainted with the blood of war, and her mountains scarred with the marks of insatiable conquest. The energy of destruction had multiplied, no longer contained within the hearts of a few but seeping into the very fabric of existence. Where once only demons had sought dominion, now even mortals wielded the power to ravage her lands.

The gods watched in sorrow as the balance tilted further, dharma now shackled by deceit, arrogance, and unrelenting bloodshed. Tridev knew that the era required more than a warrior—it needed a tactician, a savior who could weave destiny itself to ensure the survival of righteousness. Thus, Vishnu prepared to descend once more, as Krishna, the dark-skinned divine strategist, the enigma who would alter the course of history forever.

THE BIRTH OF KRISHNA – GAIA'S CHOSEN ONE

The heavens themselves shuddered when Kamsa, the tyrant king of Mathura, tightened his grip over the land. His cruelty was boundless, his paranoia endless. A prophecy had foretold his doom at the hands of the eighth child of his sister, Devaki. And so, he imprisoned her and her husband, Vasudeva, vowing to slay each child that she bore. Gaia wept at the injustice, her lands aching under the weight of Kamsa's tyranny, her rivers choked with the cries of the oppressed.

When Gaia could bear no more, when lies wrapped themselves in garlands and dharma teetered on the edge of extinction, she cried to Vishnu once more. And so, he descended—not as fire, not as storm, but as Krishna, the playful flute-bearer with a soul of thunder.

Krishna was born in the shackles of a prison, under the shadow of prophecy. Kamsa, his tyrant uncle, had turned Mathura into a fortress of fear. The Earth trembled not just beneath his armies, but beneath his cruelty.

But the divine will could not be undone. On a storm-clad midnight, the cosmos aligned, and Vishnu descended into the womb of Devaki. The prison walls glowed with an ethereal light as Krishna was born, his celestial presence a balm to the suffering earth.

Even before Krishna drew his first breath, Kamsa sought to destroy him. One by one, he slaughtered the children of his own sister, fearing the one who would end his reign. But Krishna arrived hidden, smuggled across the Yamuna by Vasudeva. The river itself parted to make way, as if Gaia whispered to her waters:

"Let him pass—he is my heartbeat."

Gaia whispered to the night, urging the winds to guide Vasudeva as he carried the newborn across the rain-lashed lands to Gokul. The Yamuna, swollen and ferocious, stilled her waters in reverence, parting to grant safe passage to the infant who bore the promise of salvation.

Raised in the pastoral embrace of Vrindavan, Krishna grew into a child of mischief and wonder. He danced on the banks of the Yamuna, playing his flute, filling the air with melodies that soothed Gaia's pain. But even as he frolicked among the gopis, he never forgot his destiny.

THE GARDEN OF GRACE: KRISHNA AND RADHA – LOVE AS GAIA'S BREATH

Before Krishna became the keeper of dharma, he was the keeper of joy.

In the meadows of Vrindavan, where the Earth still pulsed with purity, Krishna danced—not as a warrior, but as a boy whose laughter made flowers bloom.

And beside him was Radha—not just a lover, but the *mirror of Gaia's eternal longing*. She was not born of Earth. She *was* Earth—graceful, unyielding, patient.

Their love was not possession—it was union. When they danced beneath the kadamba trees, the birds paused mid-flight, the Yamuna stilled, and even the winds swirled in rhythm.

"You are the flute," Radha whispered, "and I am the breath."

"Then let us sing the world back to balance," Krishna replied.

Their love was the first healing Gaia felt. For in love—true love—there is no conquest. Only connection.

And Gaia smiled, for through Radha and Krishna, she remembered the harmony she once held.

THE SLAYING OF KAMSA – GAIA'S FIRST BALANCE RESTORED

But joy alone could not cleanse all wounds. Gaia still trembled under Kamsa's rule. Mathura, once a cradle of culture, had become a crucible of fear. The streets whispered his name like a curse. The soil darkened with the blood of innocents.

Krishna knew his dance must now become a march.

He left Vrindavan, not in secrecy, but with purpose. Radha watched him go—her eyes silent, her heart knowing.

"Where you go, the wind shall follow," she said. "But do not forget the garden within."

"Never," he smiled. "For it is the garden that gives the warrior his reason."

Krishna entered Mathura in disguise, wrapped not in armor, but in dust. The city pulsed with fear and awe. Eyes peeked from behind windows. Children pointed at the blue-skinned cowherd who walked as if he remembered every star.

Kamsa, pale behind his golden throne, summoned his wrestlers—giants bred for brute force. Krishna faced them in the arena, the crowd silent, breaths held like fragile truths.

He didn't fight. He flowed. Every movement was a dance. Every dodge, a whisper from Gaia.

When he felled the beasts, the people gasped—not in fear, but in awakening. For the first time in years, *they hoped.*

Kamsa rose, red with rage.

"I am the king! I am the sky!" he screamed.

Krishna ascended the dais slowly. He was calm. Unblinking.

"No," he said. "You are the storm. But the Earth has weathered greater."

He grabbed Kamsa, not with hatred, but with certainty. As he struck, thunder cracked—not from above, but from beneath. Gaia herself split the marble, vines crawling up the pillars.

The tyrant fell.

Flowers erupted from stone. Children wept—not for sorrow, but for release.

And Gaia sighed.

The soil of Mathura turned soft again.

But Krishna knew—this was only one wound healed. The world still spiraled toward war, and Gaia's breath grew shallower.

He looked eastward, where Kurukshetra awaited. The garden had ended.

Now, the war of dharma would begin.

THE WAR FOR DHARMA – GAIA'S LAST HOPE

The battle for balance came to its peak in Kurukshetra, where the fate of the world teetered on the edge of destruction. The Kauravas, driven by greed, had seized power unjustly, casting aside the laws of dharma. The Pandavas, rightful heirs, stood against them, but war was no longer fought with swords alone—it was waged with deception, manipulation, and an insatiable hunger for dominance. The battlefield was Gaia's greatest torment, her soil drenched in the blood of brothers, her skies thick with the cries of fallen warriors.

It was here that Krishna revealed his divine purpose. As the charioteer of Arjuna, he became the guiding force of dharma, delivering the Bhagavad Gita—the eternal truth that transcended time. "You grieve for those who should not be mourned," he declared, his voice cutting through the turmoil of doubt. "Rise, O Arjuna, for the duty of a warrior is to uphold righteousness, not to succumb to despair."

With the cosmic revelation of his Vishwaroop, Krishna unveiled his true form—a vision of infinite universes, blazing suns, and devouring time itself. Even Gaia, weary and wounded, bore witness to the vastness of his being, knowing that despite the carnage, Krishna's path was one of necessity.

THE SONG OF GAIA – THE GITA UNVEILED

Time: The stillness before the storm of Kurukshetra. Dharma breathes its last from the lips of Krishna. Gaia stands in silence—watching, waiting—as two armies prepare to sacrifice her soil for pride, revenge, and fate.

The morning of Kurukshetra arrived not with birdsong, but with tension that crackled across the field. Dust rose from chariot wheels, and conch shells groaned like ancient beasts. Between two armies stood a chariot, quiet and unmoving, where time itself had paused.

Within it, Arjuna trembled.

He looked across the field—not at strangers, but at family. Uncles, teachers, cousins, comrades—each a thread in his own soul.

His bow, Gandiva, slipped from his fingers.

"Krishna," he whispered, "my limbs fail. My mouth dries. My heart races. How can I fight them? What glory lies in slaying those I love?"

Krishna, the charioteer, said nothing. The wind fluttered his yellow cloth. His dark eyes reflected the battlefield—but deeper still, they mirrored Gaia.

"O Partha," Krishna said, voice like a river. "You mourn for those who do not deserve mourning. Yet speak as if wise. The wise do not grieve the living or the dead."

And thus began the Gita. A dialogue. A revelation. A bridge between divinity and despair.

KRISHNA SAID:

"na jayate mriyate va kadachin nayam bhutva bhavita va na bhuyaḥ ajo nityah sasvato 'yam purano na hanyate hanyamane sarire"

"The soul is never born, nor does it ever die. It has never come into being, and it will never cease to be. It is unborn, eternal, everlasting, and ancient. It is not destroyed when the body is destroyed."

Arjuna's eyes shimmered.

"But what of dharma, Krishna? If this war is fought in greed and rage, is my bow not an agent of destruction?"

Krishna smiled.

"True dharma is not inaction. It is rightful action. Gaia does not weep when leaves fall in autumn. She weeps when spring does not return."

"You are her son, Arjuna. Your hesitation wounds her more than your arrows."

GAIA'S VOICE THROUGH KRISHNA

As Krishna spoke, the earth beneath the chariot pulsed. Gaia listened—not with ears, but with roots. Every verse Krishna uttered was a balm upon her wounds. Every truth, a seed planted.

"karmaṇy-evadhikaras te ma phaleṣu kadachana ma karma-phala-hetur bhur ma te sango 'stav akarmani"

"You have the right to perform your prescribed duty, but you are not entitled to the fruits of your actions. Do not let the results be your motive, nor let your attachment be to inaction."

"To the soil that bore you, give your action. To the wind that feeds you, offer your resolve. To Gaia, offer your purity."

"yada yada hi dharmasya glanir bhavati bharata abhyutthanam adharmasya tadatmanaṁ sṛijamyaham"

"Whenever righteousness declines and unrighteousness rises, O Arjuna, I manifest myself to restore the balance."

"When the balance tilts, it is not war that Gaia fears—it is silence. It is the silence of the righteous who refuse to rise."

Arjuna gasped.

"Then Gaia is not neutral?"

Krishna looked to the horizon.

"She is never neutral. She sides always with balance. She is the battlefield, the banner, and the prayer."

"She is the bow in your hand, the fire in your chest. She is not merely beneath you. She is within you."

ARJUNA'S SURRENDER – THE AWAKENING

The warrior closed his eyes. He remembered his mother's stories. He remembered the scent of Earth after rain, the taste of water from copper pots, the shade of trees under which he trained.

"sreyah svadharmo vigunah para-dharmat sav-anusthitat svabhava-niyatam karma kurvan napnoti kilbisam"

"It is better to follow one's own dharma, even imperfectly, than to follow the dharma of another, even if perfectly performed. By performing one's own duties, one avoids sin."

"I understand," Arjuna said. "I am not killing. I am restoring. I am Gaia's warrior."

Krishna nodded.

"Then rise, O son of the Earth. Rise as Gaia's sword."

And the chariot moved. The wheels turned. The Gita echoed. And Gaia watched.

Not in fear. But in hope.

For dharma had spoken. And her son had heard.

THE FORM BEYOND FORMS

Arjuna, heart now steady, looked again at Krishna—not as a friend, not as a charioteer, but as the very pulse of the cosmos.

"Show me," he said. "Show me who you truly are."

And Krishna smiled.

"divi surya-sahasrasya bhaved yugapad utthita yadi bhaḥ sadṛsi sa syad bhasas tasya mahatmanaḥ"

"If the radiance of a thousand suns were to burst into the sky at once, it would resemble the splendor of the Supreme."

He revealed his **Vishvarupa—the Universal Form.**

Countless faces. Countless arms. Infinite weapons. Infinite eyes. Worlds revolving within him. Time, fate, birth, death—all dancing in his flames.

Gaia trembled—not in fear, but in remembrance. For this was her beginning. And perhaps, her end.

Arjuna bowed, overwhelmed.

"You are the mountain, the wind, the river, the flame. You are Gaia's soul, and I am your instrument."

"Do not fear, O warrior," Krishna said. "For even fear is born of illusion. Stand with courage. Act with love. Protect the Earth that sings through your veins."

THE ETERNAL ECHO

As the Gita unfolded, Gaia absorbed every word. Her forests carried the sound through their leaves. Her rivers murmured the verses into every drop.

Krishna had not just taught a prince. He had healed the Earth.

The dialogue between him and Arjuna was no longer just a lesson. It was a seed—planted in time. A hymn that would echo across centuries.

In the stillness of temples. In the rustling of leaves. In the courage of the just. In the silence of meditation.

The Gita lives. Not only in scriptures. But in Gaia herself.

The chariot rolled on. The war awaited. But now, Arjuna did not fear.

He had become a flame that walked. And Gaia, his mother, had found her son again.

The war of Kurukshetra raged, leaving devastation in its wake, but dharma was restored. The Kauravas fell, and the Pandavas, though victorious, were forever changed.

THE DEPARTURE OF KRISHNA – THE END OF AN AGE

But no avatar remains forever. And even the melody of the Gita must find its silence.

Years after the battle faded, and the blood of Kurukshetra had dried into dust, Krishna walked alone under the twilight sky. The sun no longer glowed golden—it hung low and weary, like Gaia herself.

In the forest of Prabhas, far from the throne and the war-cries, Krishna sat beneath a tree, his flute silent, his heart full.

A hunter, blinded by fate, mistook the gentle curve of Krishna's foot for a deer and released his arrow. It struck—not a beast, but the body that had once held the cosmos.

Krishna fell—not with pain, but with peace. Gaia caught him. Her arms, made of soil and song, cradled the avatar like a mother welcoming her son.

"You have carried me," she whispered. "Now let me carry you."

And as his breath slowed, the wind stilled, the trees bowed, and the riverbanks wept.

With Krishna's passing, the Dvapara Yuga dimmed. His footprints faded into myth, but his voice still echoed in Gaia's core.

The flute was silent. But its tune lingered.

DWARKA – THE SUNKEN CITY OF GRACE AND GLORY

Krishna's kingdom, the celestial city of Dwarka, once rose from the sea like a lotus of light. Its towers kissed the clouds. Its streets shimmered with virtue. It was a city not merely built on stone—but on values.

Gaia held it like a crown.

But after the avatar's departure, it began to sink—not just into water, but into legend. The oceans rose, as if mourning his exit. The waves swallowed marble and memory alike.

Today, the ruins of Dwarka lie beneath the Arabian Sea, off the coast of Gujarat. Divers return with tales of submerged structures—pillars, walls, anchors. Proof, perhaps, that glory built in time cannot escape the laws of time.

"Nothing is eternal," Gaia whispers. "Not kingdoms, not kings. Not even avatars."

And so, Dwarka became Gaia's message to the world— A warning in the form of a wonder. A lesson carved in coral and coraline silence.

Nothing lasts. Except the consequences of our choices.

Chapter 10

THE BUDDHA AVATAR AND THE WRATH OF KALI YUGA

"बुद्धं शरणं गच्छामि।
कालिदोषे प्रबुद्धं जीवनम्॥"

"To the Enlightened One I surrender; amidst the darkness of time, awakening dawns."

10

THE WRATH OF KALI YUGA

Time: The silent edge of Dvapara, where chaos still rumbles but introspection begins to stir. Dharma, weary of bloodshed, now hides in forests and caves. Gaia breathes in solitude, aching not for warriors, but for wisdom. The world, heavy with noise, begins to crave silence.

As the twilight of Dvapara Yuga faded, the shadows of greed and arrogance stretched further, consuming the hearts of men. The sacred rivers, once teeming with purity, grew tainted with avarice. The forests, Gaia's lush tresses, were slashed and burned, reduced to barren wastelands. Mountains wept as their veins of gold and minerals were plundered to feed human excess.

Gaia's agony surged through the cosmos, and the gods watched with sorrow as her once-pristine form bore the scars of mankind's unchecked hunger.

The arrival of Kali Yuga marked the dawn of devastation unlike any before. The age of darkness, where dharma stood on a single fractured limb, had begun. Mankind had grown reckless, detached from nature's rhythm. Cities of opulence rose on the graves of ancient trees, and rivers choked under the weight of poison and filth. The earth, once a giver of abundance, struggled to sustain those who had forgotten to respect her.

Gaia, in her anguish, cried out to the heavens, but her voice was drowned by the clamor of war, deception, and unchecked desires.

The Tridev—Brahma, Vishnu, and Shiva—watched in despair.

"The balance is lost," Brahma murmured, gazing upon Gaia's wounded form. "Mankind has forsaken harmony."

Vishnu, the eternal preserver, looked upon his beloved creation with sorrow. "Greed has become their guiding force. Their souls grow restless, enslaved by material desires. They do not listen to the cries of their own mother."

Shiva, the destroyer, clenched his jaw. "If they will not heed her pain, then they shall taste her fury."

And fury she unleashed.

Gaia trembled, her rage unshackled. The oceans swelled, consuming cities in towering waves. Earthquakes shattered the ground, swallowing entire civilizations. Mountains crumbled, forests ignited, and the air grew thick with the smoke of humanity's own ruin.

The pandemic of disease – Cholera, swept through nations, striking down the mighty and the weak alike, leaving only despair in its wake. The world writhed, a mother scorned, punishing her children for their arrogance.

Amidst this turmoil, Vishnu chose his next descent—not as a warrior, not as a king, but as a seeker of truth. He took form as Siddhartha Gautama, the Buddha, the awakened one.

Born into a world of wealth and luxury, Siddhartha had everything but peace. He saw suffering—of the old, the sick, and the dying—and felt an ache deep within his soul. He walked away from his kingdom, from power, from all material attachments, in search of a path that could lead mankind away from its endless cycle of destruction.

Under the Bodhi tree, as he meditated, Gaia whispered to him. "They do not hear me," she lamented. "They trample upon my body, strip me bare, and leave me to bleed. They seek salvation in wealth, in power, but they do not seek balance."

Buddha opened his eyes, his mind illuminated. "Then I shall teach them."

He walked across lands, his presence serene amidst the chaos of the world. He spoke of harmony, of moderation, of dharma beyond rituals and blind faith. He taught that greed was the root of suffering, that detachment was the key to liberation, and that true enlightenment lay in kindness, in balance, in the understanding that all life was intertwined.

For a time, Gaia breathed easier. The rivers whispered his wisdom, the winds carried his words, and the land sighed with momentary relief. But mankind's nature, ever restless, soon forgot.

Temples of stone replaced the sacred groves. Greed found new forms—conquest, industry, excess. Gaia's torment worsened. The sky turned grey, choked with the filth of progress. The oceans churned, spewing poison back upon the land. She had warned, she had pleaded, she had given wisdom, but mankind refused to listen.

Vishnu, in his enlightened form, watched as humanity once again slid into its own ruin. He turned his gaze to the heavens, where the Tridev stood in silence.

"They will not stop," Buddha whispered. "Their hunger knows no bounds."

Shiva's voice rumbled like a storm. "Then they shall face the consequence of their own making." And so, Gaia prepares for her final reckoning.

Tsunamis rise from her depths, earthquakes shake her core, storms tear through her skies. Pandemics come and go, a mere taste of the sorrow she has suffered. The warnings have been given. The balance is near its breaking point.

And as the age of Kali rages on, the gods watch in silence, awaiting the final descent—the Tenth Avatar, Kalki, the destroyer of corruption, the harbinger of Gaia's last cleansing.

The end is yet to come, and with it, the fate of all creation.

🌍 GAIA'S WAITING

"THE EARTH STILL LISTENS"

Not all tales are of the past. Some are maps of return.

THE AWAKENING OF KALI YUGA: GAIA'S SAINTS ACROSS TIME

As Kali Yuga advanced, Gaia stood wounded—not just by war, but by the indifference of mankind. The Earth bore wounds not carved by weapons, but by greed, ignorance, and arrogance. Her rivers no longer flowed with joy, but with pollutants. Her forests did not hum in harmony—they gasped for breath.

She whispered again to the heavens.

"Let them remember. Let them hear truth in human voices."

And so, Vishnu answered—not through singular avatars, but through enlightened souls, prophets, and saints who would rise in every corner of the Earth. These were not kings or conquerors, but seekers, wanderers, and preachers—born to awaken, guide, and return humanity to the divine pulse of Gaia.

Mahavira, the twenty-fourth Tirthankara of Jainism, came forth as the first voice. Born into royalty, he gave it all away to embrace stillness. He walked barefoot over scorching stone and thorned paths, teaching *ahimsa*—not merely as abstinence from violence, but as a deep acknowledgment that all life is Gaia's breath.

"To harm another," he said, "is to harm the breath of Earth itself."

He rejected indulgence, practiced intense penance, and treated insects and birds with equal reverence. Through silence and simplicity, he offered a blueprint for minimalism—one where man took only what was needed and gave back twice as much.

Jesus Christ, born in Bethlehem, was Gaia's heartbeat made flesh. He walked with fishermen and sat with lepers, his feet caked with soil and love. He reminded mankind that salvation lay not in golden structures but in kindness and compassion.

"Blessed are the meek," he whispered. "For they shall inherit the Earth."

He turned water into wine, not to dazzle, but to demonstrate that divinity could infuse the most elemental parts of creation. He was crucified upon wood, symbolizing Gaia's pain at the hands of ignorance. But even from the cross, he forgave.

"Forgive them," he said, "for they know not what they do."

And Gaia wept. Not for his suffering, but for the suffering he chose to bear on her behalf.

Prophet Muhammad emerged from the arid sands of Arabia. In the stillness of a cave, the divine voice returned to Earth. He taught of balance—between the material and the spiritual, between indulgence and gratitude.

"Do not waste water," he said, "even if you perform ablution on the banks of a flowing river."

He invited humanity to recognize that Earth is sacred, and so is every act done upon it. His teachings on justice, charity, and humility reinvigorated a broken society, stitching it back with threads of discipline and collective good.

Gaia, too, found solace in his words. For he taught his people to walk gently on her soil.

Guru Nanak Dev, born in the fields of Punjab, listened to the wind, watched the rivers, and heard Gaia sing.

"Pavan Guru, Pani Pita, Mata Dharat Mahat," he said. "Air is the teacher, water the father, and Earth the great mother."

He broke bread with the untouchables, drank from streams with the downtrodden. His verses, the Guru Granth Sahib, became hymns not just of divinity, but of ecological harmony. To him, every being was part of one divine song.

"There is no Hindu. There is no Muslim," he declared. "There is only the light of Gaia in all."

Chaitanya Mahaprabhu, born in Bengal, was Gaia's river turned dancer. His limbs moved like waves, his voice rose like monsoon winds, and his ecstasy became a spiritual cyclone.

"Chant the name," he called, "and dissolve into her rhythm."

He reminded humanity that devotion was not passive. It was thunderous, alive, and kinetic. Through kirtans and gatherings under trees, he reawakened Bhakti—not as a path of escape, but as a dance with Gaia herself.

Sri Ramakrishna, in a quiet Dakshineswar temple, sat before a goddess carved from stone—but saw her breathe.

"All paths lead to her," he said. "The Divine Mother, the source of all."

He did not preach a new religion. He embraced them all. Through silence, contemplation, and childlike innocence, he demonstrated that Gaia was both mother and mirror.

He said, "Money is earth, and earth is money," reminding people that the material world is not evil—it is sacred, but it must be respected.

His greatest contribution was perhaps not his own voice—but his awakening of another.

Swami Vivekananda, fierce as fire and calm as sky, rose from Ramakrishna's blessings like an eagle from a storm. He spoke not only to Indians, but to the world.

"Arise, awake, and stop not until the goal is reached," he thundered.

In Chicago, he stood before the world and declared all men divine. He called for harmony—not just among religions, but with the cosmos itself.

He spoke of service, discipline, and unity.

"They alone live who live for others," he cried.

And Gaia smiled. For in his voice, she heard both resolve and reverence.

Mother Teresa, born far from the Ganges, became the river of compassion in Kolkata's heart. Where Gaia was most scarred—in gutters, in orphanages, in diseased beds—she walked barefoot.

"Do small things with great love," she whispered, brushing away flies, holding broken hands.

She never preached. She only touched. She never judged. She only served.

Through her, Gaia healed quietly—one soul at a time.

GAIA'S WHISPER IN THE MODERN WORLD

But what of now? What of this moment where glaciers melt like memories, forests fall like empires, and silence is no longer meditative—but suffocating?

Gaia watches as plastic chokes rivers, as machines scar her skin. But she still hopes. Still whispers.

~ In children planting trees. In women guarding forests. In farmers choosing organic. In youth marching for climate. In scientists weaving solar into sky. In poets who write not for applause—but for awareness.

She stirs in slow revolutions. Not in palaces—but in kitchen gardens, village collectives, reclaimed oceans, and rooftops turned green.

She no longer waits for avatars. She calls *you*.

"You are my saints now," she whispers. "You are my disciples. My limbs. My breath."

Every act of care is a hymn. Every seed sown is a scripture. Every tear for nature is a ritual.

The age of seers is not over. It has just begun—within us.

And so, the saints shall rise—not in robes or thunder, but in recycling bins, in reforested hills, in hands that mend, and hearts that refuse to forget.

Gaia waits, yes. But now, she waits *with us*.

Let your story be the next verse in her eternal hymn.

THE GIFT OF THE LEGENDS

"NOT TO WORSHIP, BUT TO AWAKEN"

The gods walked to remind us that we are divine, too.

GAIA'S AWAKENING IN KALI YUGA

As the ages passed, mankind's greed knew no bounds. Gaia, once lush and vibrant, lay ravaged and wounded.

Her forests were stripped bare, her oceans poisoned, her creatures driven to extinction. The sky choked with smoke, and the winds howled with sorrow.

She wept, but no one listened. Then, she roared.

The earth trembled with quakes, swallowing cities whole. The oceans surged in tsunamis, reclaiming what was stolen. The winds screamed through hurricanes, tearing down the towers of arrogance. Disease spread like fire, a silent plague reminding mankind of its frailty. COVID was not a curse—it was a warning.

The Tridev watched in sorrow. "We gave them wisdom, and they cast it aside," Brahma sighed. "They poisoned the mother who bore them," Vishnu murmured.

"They shall reap what they have sown," Shiva declared, his third eye burning with divine fury. Thus, the final cycle had begun. Gaia's patience had ended. The age of reckoning was upon them. Would mankind rise from the ashes, or would they perish in the storm they had created?

The choice is & always was theirs!!! (***Tesam eva chayanam, sada eva tat asit***)

◕ 🌱 ✦ Chapter 11

THE LAST VERSE: THE SEED OF SATYAYUGA

"बीजं सत्ययुगस्य त्वमेव।
पुनः आरभ्यते सृष्टिः, त्वद्विवेकेन॥"

"You are the seed of the new Satya Yuga; creation begins again through your wisdom."

"Rise, Not as One—But as Many"

Gaia's heroes no longer wear crowns. They wear courage.

11

THE LAST VERSE – THE SEED OF SATYAYUGA

Time: The breath of now. A sacred pause between despair and dawn. Between the echoes of myth and the emergence of meaning. Gaia, our eternal witness, listens still.

It began with stories. Told not from books, but from breath. Whispered beneath banyan trees, sung beside the flames of winter fires, passed from the tongues of elders to the hearts of children. These were not tales. They were time itself—woven into lullabies, chants, and the silences between.

Mythology was not read. It was received. Like sunlight to leaf. Like rain to parched earth.

Once, stories were sacred threads that stitched humanity to nature. But now, the stories sleep. And Gaia dreams alone.

Yet not all is lost.

This journey—this epic of yugas and incarnations, of oceans parted and demons slain, of sages and saviors, of Gaia and god—was never a tale of the past. It is a map. A mirror. A memory of who we were meant to be.

Because today, Gaia still waits. And now, she waits for you.

THE GIFT OF THE LEGENDS

The avatars did not come to dominate. They came to dissolve illusion. They wore mortal form to show us that divinity lies not in distance, but in devotion.

Rama carried the weight of law, so we might learn integrity. Sita walked through fire, so we might understand purity. Krishna held the cosmos in his eyes, and whispered purpose to the lost. Narasimha tore through arrogance to protect the innocent. The Buddha sat in silence, and the world learned to listen again.

Each of them, a flame. Each of them, a reflection of Gaia's hope.

The Earth you stand on is not cracked—it is consecrated. Blessed by the presence of those who bled so we might bloom.

Kneel if you must. Cry if you feel. But know this—

The torch is no longer in hands of god. It is in your hands.

YOU ARE THE AVATAR NOW

Kali Yuga spins on, a storm of forgetting. But the age of waiting is over. No Kalki shall come galloping unless we rise to saddle the horse.

The time of one avatar is past. This is the age of awakening within many.

The orphan tending to wounded animals. The woman building a school from mud. The scientist planting forests with drones. The artist painting gods into graffiti. The coder translating Gita into 100 languages. The student who questions not just for grades, but for truth—and stands up for what's right in the classroom and beyond. The parent who raises children with kindness over conquest, and plants the seed of values before ambition. The professional who chooses ethics over profit, weaving purpose into every project. The industrialist who transforms factories into green sanctuaries, making sustainability more sacred than scale. The politician who listens not to applause, but to the cry of the voiceless, and leads not for votes—but for vision.

These are the avatars Gaia watches now. These are her warriors.

Not with swords. But with seeds. Not in war cries. But in whispers that restore.

You. Me. All of us. Together.

We are no longer waiting for change. We are the change.

🌐 One Humanity

"Borders Fade. Dharma Remains."

The Earth is one home. We are one tribe

ONE HUMANITY, ONE MESSAGE

We have worshipped in different ways. Spoken in different tongues. Lived under different skies.

But now—now we must remember the first and final religion: Humanity.

This is the spirit of Vasudhaiva Kutumbakam—the whole world is one family.

वसुधैव कुटुम्बकम् *"The Earth is but one household".*

It is no longer a metaphor. It is a manifesto.

The place of worship of tomorrow are not made of stone. They are made of acts.

In the age of AI, we have no barriers of language. In the age of virtual bridges, we have no borders of thought.

Let the story of Gaia be coded into every cloud. Let her cry be streamed into every home. Let her whisper reach every screen.

"Return to balance." "Live as one tribe—Earthlings." "Speak not of salvation. Speak of service."

Now is not the time to forget. Now is the time to merge.

🜋 *Return to Roots*

"Modernity Must Remember"

Let innovation be rooted. Let progress bow to purpose.

GO BACK TO THE ROOTS

Rebuild, yes. But rebuild upon memory. Innovate, yes. But innovate with wisdom. Accelerate, yes. But never without anchoring.

Let us create cities that breathe. Machines that protect. Governments that serve. Communities that heal.

Go back to trees as ancestors. Go back to rivers as veins. Go back to song as scripture. Go back to one another—as kin.

When greed dissolves, When power bows, When knowledge humbles, When innovation listens—

Then the wheel shall turn again. And Satyayuga shall not descend from the clouds. It will rise—from our roots. From Gaia's womb and your will.

THE TIME IS NOW

The legends have offered their legacy. The avatars have cleared the path.

Now the next verse is yours to sing. Write not with ink. Write with intention. Speak not with tongue. Speak with action.

Let this book not be the final chapter. Let it be your call to arms. To rise. To remember. To restore.

Gaia still sings. Can you hear her?

Then rise, O child of Dharma.

For the Yuga of Awakening begins with you.

"Uttistha dharmasya putra! Jagratah yugastha prarambha tabyi sthita"

🕊️ *Epilogue – Gaia's Guardians*

"From Myth to Manifesto"

No more waiting. The chorus of avatars has begun.

EPILOGUE: THE AWAKENING OF GAIA'S GUARDIANS

Time: The cusp of transformation. As the echoes of yugas fade into modern frequencies, Gaia opens her eyes once more.

She has watched empires rise like tides and crumble like sandcastles. She has seen gods descend, saints awaken, civilizations flourish—and fall. She remembers the touch of Rama's feet, the weight of Krishna's silence, the warmth of Sita's return. But never before has Gaia trembled beneath such a weight as now.

This is not the burden of stone, nor steel. It is the weight of neglect, of disconnection, of humanity's unravelling from nature's thread.

Where once the avatars came to balance the scales, today the balance tips further. And so, Gaia does not call for a savior. She calls for a chorus.

We stand on the brink—not just of environmental collapse, but of *spiritual amnesia*. The air thickens, oceans rise, and forests fall not to demons, but to decisions. And amidst it all, Gaia asks not for devotion— but for responsibility.

Nations once obsessed with borders now awaken to an unrelenting truth—*no wall can hold back a flood, no weapon can cool a warming sky*. The battles of today will not be won with swords, but with empathy, innovation, and unshakable resolve.

And in this theater of reckoning, a new generation rises:

Not soldiers of conquest, but stewards of creation. Not kings in palaces, but children with questions. Not prophets from mountains, but citizens with vision.

The avatars of old once descended to restore balance; now, their mantle passes to a new generation.

The world stands at the precipice of an epochal shift. Nations, long fixated on fortifying their borders, now awaken to a greater truth: no fortress is impenetrable when the very foundation of existence crumbles. The protectors of today are not warriors of conquest but stewards of renewal, champions of an Earth gasping for reprieve. The seas rise, the forests burn, and the air thickens with the residue of human excess. The time for idle lamentation has passed—Gaia demands action.

Society, once fractured by the illusions of caste, creed, and faith, begins to remember a forgotten song—a song of unity, woven into the essence of all living things. The avatars once walked among men, their teachings scattered like seeds in the wind. Now, those seeds awaken in the hearts of those who dare to see beyond the illusions of division. One religion remains, one unwavering faith: humanity. The walls we built in our minds dissolve, making way for a singular, unshakable truth—existence is shared, and so too must be its salvation.

Yet, in the grand theater of change, corporations hold the pen that writes the fate of tomorrow. For too long, they have charted a course dictated by profit alone, blind to the symphony of nature's warning. But there is hope. A new paradigm emerges—not one of mere compliance, but of conscious reformation. No longer is sustainability an afterthought; it is the foundation upon which industries must be reborn. The architects of commerce must now become architects of harmony, wielding innovation as their instrument and responsibility as their creed. The age of extractive business fades; the dawn of regenerative enterprise begins.

And so, the avatars rise—not as celestial beings descending from divine realms, but as those who dare to dream differently, to act decisively, to lead fearlessly. They are the thinkers and the builders, the policymakers and the rebels, the poets and the pragmatists. They are the awakened—Gaia's guardians, moving in unison with the heartbeat of the Earth.

The story does not end here, for stories of true transformation are never finite. Instead, this is the threshold of an awakening, the moment before the tide turns. The wind carries whispers of change, the rivers hum with renewal, and the earth trembles—not in fear, but in anticipation.

Gaia watches, Gaia waits.

The question is no longer who will answer the call.

GLOSSARY OF MYTHOLOGICAL REFERENCES

Gaia – A symbolic representation of Earth as a divine feminine energy, mother of all creation, and soul of balance.

Yuga – The great ages in Hindu cosmology. Satya Yuga (age of truth), Treta Yuga, Dvapara Yuga, and Kali Yuga (age of darkness).

Avatars – Divine incarnations of Vishnu, born to restore cosmic balance and protect dharma.

Dharma – Righteousness, duty, truth, and moral order that sustains life and creation.

Matsya – The fish incarnation that saved ancient scriptures and humanity from a great flood.

Kurma – The tortoise avatar that supported the churning of the ocean of milk.

Varaha – The boar avatar who rescued Earth (Bhudevi) from cosmic waters.

Narasimha – The half-man, half-lion form that destroyed the demon Hiranyakashipu.

Vamana – The dwarf avatar who subdued King Bali with cosmic steps.

Rama – The warrior-king of Ayodhya, embodiment of truth and justice.

Sita – Incarnation of Gaia and divine feminine, consort of Rama.

Krishna – The flute-bearing avatar who guided Arjuna and revealed the Bhagavad Gita.

Radha – The eternal beloved of Krishna, representing divine love and the soul's longing.

Buddha – The enlightened one, whose silence and wisdom transformed suffering.

Kalki – The final avatar prophesied to end Kali Yuga and restore Satya Yuga.

Kurukshetra – The great battlefield where the Mahabharata and the Bhagavad Gita unfold.

Bhagavad Gita – A sacred dialogue between Krishna and Arjuna, the essence of dharma and spiritual wisdom.

Dwarka – The glorious city built by Krishna, later submerged by the sea, symbol of impermanence.

Vasudhaiva Kutumbakam – A Sanskrit phrase meaning "The world is one family."

Satyayuga – The age of truth, the first and purest era in the cycle of yugas, marked by harmony and virtue.

🔥❀ REFLECTIVE READER'S NOTE – A FLAME YOU NOW CARRY

"दीपं ज्वालय, पन्थानं दर्शय।
त्वमेव अवतारः– इदानीं॥"

"Light the flame, reveal the path. You are the Avatar—now."

READER'S NOTE – A FLAME YOU NOW CARRY

✨ Final Reader's Note

"You Carry the Flame Now"

Let this not be the last word. Let it be your first act

If these pages stirred something within you—if they made your heart ache, your spine straighten, your breath deepen—then you have heard her. Gaia has spoken, not through thunder, but through this quiet chorus of forgotten truths.

Let this not be a book you place upon a shelf. Let it be a song you carry into the world.

You are not the reader. You are the continuation.

Take what you've remembered here. Share it. Sing it to your children. Code it into your creations. Paint it on your walls. Plant it into the earth.

Become the living page. The walking hymn. And may the verses you write next be blessed by Gaia herself.

LIST OF REFERENCES & INSPIRATIONS

1. **The Bhagavad Gita** – Sacred scripture from the Mahabharata, central to Krishna's teachings and the foundation of dharma explored in this work.

2. **Srimad Bhagavatam (Bhagavata Purana)** – Text detailing the Dashavatara (ten avatars) of Lord Vishnu and their divine interventions.

3. **The Ramayana** – Epic describing the life of Lord Rama and Sita, serving as the cornerstone for the values of truth, sacrifice, and divine duty.

4. **The Mahabharata** – Ancient epic providing the context for the Kurukshetra war, the Gita, and the trials of dharma in Dvapara Yuga.

5. **Maha Upanishad** – Source of the verse "Vasudhaiva Kutumbakam" – the Earth is one family.

6. **Vedic Cosmology** – Concepts of the four Yugas (Satya, Treta, Dvapara, Kali) and cyclical time.

7. **Mythological and Archaeological Interpretations** – Including the tale and

submerged ruins of Dwarka, referenced in modern marine archaeology.

8. **Teachings of Saints and Sages** – Life lessons and insights from Ramakrishna Paramhansa, Swami Vivekananda, Chaitanya Mahaprabhu, Mahavira, Buddha, Guru Nanak Dev, Prophet Muhammad, Jesus Christ, and Mother Teresa.

9. **Modern Ecological Thought** – Philosophies connecting myth to nature from figures like Vandana Shiva, Satish Kumar, and the global sustainability movement.

10. **Environmental Science and Climate Reports** – References to floods, fires, rising sea levels, and global warming as signs of imbalance.

11. **Contemporary Spiritual Literature** – Works connecting mythology to environmental awareness and human consciousness evolution.

12. **Artistic and Cultural Narratives** – Elements of folk storytelling, bedtime mythology, oral tradition, and philosophical commentary passed through generations.

AUTHOR'S DISCLAIMER

This book is a work of fiction and creative nonfiction rooted in the public domain traditions of Hindu, Jain, Buddhist, and global spiritual philosophies. The author has drawn upon public domain scriptures such as the *Bhagavad Gita, Ramayana, Mahabharata, Srimad Bhagavatam*, and *Upanishads* for inspiration and interpretation. Any translated Sanskrit verses presented are original renderings by the author unless otherwise noted.

Historical and religious figures such as Buddha, Jesus Christ, Prophet Muhammad, Guru Nanak, and others are referenced with respect and poetic license, and their teachings are portrayed in alignment with public domain understanding or oral traditions.

No copyrighted material, text, or imagery from third-party authors or publications has been knowingly used. All modern thinkers and environmental themes referenced are acknowledged solely as philosophical inspiration, without reproducing any protected content.

The rights to this book and its original content, including text and thematic interpretation, belong solely to the author. Unauthorized reproduction or use of this material is prohibited without prior written consent.

SUMMARY

GAIA: THE ETERNAL MOTHER, THE WOUNDED GUARDIAN

In the ancient echoes of creation, she was the first breath of existence, the heartbeat of the universe—Gaia, the sacred mother of all life. She is not merely earth; she is consciousness woven into the very fabric of being, a spirit so ancient that even time bows before her presence. To the wise sages of the Vedas, she is *Bhūmi Devi*, the nurturer, the foundation of all life, the ever-giving force of existence. To the Hellenic poets, she was Gaia, the primal deity from whom the Titans and gods emerged, the great sustainer of Olympus and the world alike.

Both in the scriptures of the East and the myths of the West, Gaia is the eternal feminine—the life-giver and the harbinger of justice. The Greeks envisioned her as the all-seeing mother, the great unyielding force that bore the heavens and cradled the seas. In the Vedic hymns, she is inseparable from the cosmic order, protected by Vishnu and Shiva, the embodiment of harmony and destruction alike. She is the mother of mountains and rivers, the womb from which gods and mortals alike take form, and the sorrowed guardian who has watched her children betray her again and again.

Her voice is in the whisper of the wind, her sorrow in the crashing waves, and her rage in the fire that consumes civilizations. Across yugas, she has endured, bestowing blessings upon those who revere her and unleashing calamity upon those who defile her. The great Titans of Greece and the Asuras of Bharat both sought to challenge her dominion, only to fall before the inevitability of her will. And as humanity marches into its final age—Kali Yuga—her patience wears thin.

She has wept for too long.

Now, she rises.

A NEW AGE OF GAIA'S GUARDIANS

The avatars of this age are not mythical beings; they are the policymakers, the activists, the corporate leaders, and the everyday individuals who dare to challenge the status quo. Each of us holds the power to be an agent of change—to rewrite the narrative of destruction and give rise to an era of harmony. If we honor the legacy of Gaia, if we heed the lessons of avatars past, we will usher in a new world—not one defined by borders, divisions, or short-term profits, but one where humanity, industry, and nature exist in sustainable unity.

The call has been made. Will we answer?

GLOSSARY OF TERMS

A

Adharma – The decline or absence of dharma (cosmic order); chaos or unrighteousness.

Amrit – Nectar of immortality, retrieved from the churning of the cosmic ocean.

Asura – Beings often opposed to the Devas, symbolizing ego, power, or imbalance.

Avatar – A divine incarnation taken by Vishnu to restore balance during different Yugas.

Ayodhya – The sacred kingdom of Rama, representing dharma and order.

B

Bhumi Devi / Gaia – Personification of Earth as a divine mother and living consciousness.

Brahma – The Creator among the Tridev (trinity), responsible for the birth of the universe.

Brahmin – The priestly class in Vedic tradition, often the preservers of sacred knowledge.

D

Dharma – Righteousness, cosmic duty, or natural law; the principle sustaining harmony.

Dashavatara – The ten major incarnations of Vishnu across the Yugas to restore balance.

Deva – Celestial beings or gods upholding dharma.

G

Ganga – Sacred river flowing from Shiva's jata, symbol of purification and divine descent.

Garuda – Vishnu's mount; often symbolizes swift divine intervention.

H

Hayagriva – Demon who stole the Vedas, defeated by Matsya.

Hiranyaksha – Asura who plunged Earth into the abyss, defeated by Varaha.

Hiranyakashipu – Tyrant who defied the gods; slain by Narasimha.

J

Jata – Shiva's matted locks, symbolic of controlled chaos and spiritual energy.

Janaka – King of Mithila and foster father of Sita, a symbol of wisdom and dharmic rule.

K

Kali Yuga – The current age of decline, marked by moral decay and disconnection from nature.

Kurma – The tortoise avatar of Vishnu, who supported the cosmic churning.

L

Lakshmi – Goddess of abundance and beauty, emerged from the cosmic ocean during Samudra Manthan.

Lanka – Island kingdom ruled by Ravana, destroyed during Rama's avatar.

M

Matsya – The fish avatar who rescued the Vedas and guided Manu through the deluge.

Mohini – Vishnu's enchanting female form used to distribute Amrit and deceive the Asuras.

Mount Mandara – Used as the churning rod during Samudra Manthan.

N

Narasimha – The man-lion avatar who destroyed Hiranyakashipu at dusk on the threshold.

Nagas – Serpent beings, associated with cosmic energy and often guardians of treasures.

P

Parashurama – The axe-wielding warrior sage avatar who punished corrupt Kshatriyas.

Prahlada – Devotee of Vishnu and son of Hiranyakashipu, protected by divine grace.

R

Rama – Avatar of Vishnu symbolizing ideal kingship and dharma in action.

Ravana – Ten-headed king of Lanka; embodiment of ego, abducted Sita, slain by Rama.

Rishi – Seer or sage, a bearer of divine knowledge and guidance.

S

Satyayuga – The golden age of truth, purity, and spiritual harmony.

Samudra Manthan – The churning of the ocean by Devas and Asuras to obtain Amrit.

Sita – Avatar of Bhumi/Gaia, wife of Rama, and symbol of divine grace and resilience.

T

Tridev – The holy trinity: Brahma (Creator), Vishnu (Preserver), Shiva (Destroyer).

Treta Yuga – The age after Satya Yuga, marked by growing ego and decline of dharma.

V

Varaha – The boar avatar who lifted Gaia from the cosmic ocean.

Vamana – The dwarf avatar who humbled King Bali with three cosmic strides.

Vedas – Ancient scriptures embodying knowledge, wisdom, and dharmic codes.

Vishnu – The Preserver among the Tridev, manifests in avatars to maintain balance.

Y

Yajna – Sacred Vedic ritual; offering to gods in the form of fire sacrifices.

Yuga – Epoch or age in Hindu cosmology: Satya, Treta, Dvapara, Kali.